As she glanced backward, Lily's eyes went automatically to his chest. Beneath the dark, slightly crumpled jacket of his perfectly tailored suit, his white shirt was untucked, the collar open, lopsided, showing an expanse of deep golden flesh and one sculpted collarbone.

She wasn't sure which was worse—the instant rush of hot, indignant anger because the kiss that had turned her inside out with longing had been given so casually, so randomly, by a man whose body was barely cold from another woman's bed.

Or the low-down ache of desire and the shameful knowledge that she didn't care. That she just wanted to kiss him again.

India Grey

THE SOCIETY WIFE

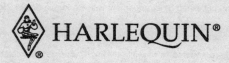

TORONTO • NEW YORK • LONDON
AMSTERDAM • PARIS • SYDNEY • HAMBURG
STOCKHOLM • ATHENS • TOKYO • MILAN • MADRID
PRAGUE • WARSAW • BUDAPEST • AUCKLAND

Recycling programs
for this product may
not exist in your area.

ISBN-13: 978-0-373-12967-6

THE SOCIETY WIFE

First North American Publication 2011

Copyright © 2009 by India Grey

This edition published by arrangement with Harlequin Books S.A.

For questions and comments about the quality of this book
please contact us at Customer_eCare@Harlequin.ca.

® and TM are trademarks of the publisher. Trademarks indicated with ® are registered in the United States Patent and Trademark Office, the Canadian Trade Marks Office and in other countries.

www.eHarlequin.com

Printed in U.S.A.

THE SOCIETY WIFE

CHAPTER ONE

THE shadow of the helicopter fell over the lush velvet lawns of Stowell Castle, stirring up the hot August air and ruffling the canopies of the great trees in the parkland.

Tristan Romero de Losada Montalvo glanced down. Below him the party was already well under way, and he could see waiters carrying trays of champagne circulating between the groups of outlandishly dressed guests scattered across the emerald grass. Dispassionately he noticed that people were looking up, emerging from the marquees placed at opposite ends of the lawn and shielding their eyes from the sinking sun to watch his arrival.

It was set to be the party of the year, because Tom Montague's Annual Charity Costume Ball always was. This was the event that drew the glitterati and the aristos back from their Malibu beach houses and Tuscan palazzos to indulge in twenty-four hours of lavish hedonism in the idyllic setting of Stowell Castle's gardens.

It was also the event that had drawn Tristan Romero back from the jaws of hell some two thousand miles away, for reasons that had nothing to do with indulgence or hedonism.

He was here for Tom.

Sighing wearily, he circled the helicopter round over the lawn so that the roofs of the marquees snapped and strained like galleons' sails. Tom Montague was the seventh Earl of Cotebrook and one of the most genuinely good and generous people imaginable; a combination which Tristan felt was particularly dangerous—especially where women were concerned. Tom only ever looked for the good in people, even when it was invisible to the rest of humankind. Which was why they'd been friends for such a long time, Tristan thought acidly, and why he now felt duty bound to come and make sure that the girl that Tom had talked about incessantly over the past few weeks was worthy of him.

But, of course, he would be dishonest as well as emotionally bankrupt if he tried to pretend that that was his only reason for coming.

Ultimately he was here because the tabloid press and the paparazzi and the gossip columnists expected him to be. It was part of the deal he had made when he sold his soul to the devil. Grimly he swung the helicopter round, following the path of the river that looped around Stowell and marked its northern boundary. As he came lower his eyes raked the trees along the river bank, looking for the telltale glitter of sunlight on a long lens.

They would be there, of that he was sure. One of the hardened group of paparazzi elite, who were dedicated enough to go the extra distance for a picture and ruthless enough not to question the ethics of getting it. They would be there somewhere, watching and waiting.

He would be almost insulted if they weren't. Many people in a similar position to him complained endlessly about press intrusion, but to Tristan that was missing the point. It was a game. A game of strategy and skill, in which the truth was an irrelevance and a lapse of concentration could cost you your reputation. Tristan didn't like the paparazzi, but neither did he underestimate them for a second. It was simply a case of use or be used. Be the manipulator or the victim.

And Tristan Romero would never be a victim again.

Down below Lily Alexander slipped through the crowds of people in their spectacular costumes as if in a dream. The champagne in her hand was vintage, the silk Grecian-style dress she wore was designer, and the stretch of grass beneath her bare feet was at that moment just about the most enviable place to be on the planet.

So why did she feel as if something was missing?

There was a saying on the London modelling circuit: 'There are three things that money can't buy: love, happiness and an invitation to the Stowell Annual Costume Ball.' *Magical* was the word people used to describe it, in tones of wistful reverence. Lily was unutterably privileged to be here, as she told herself for about the fortieth time that evening, blotting out the dissatisfied little voice that answered, *But where's the magic? Surely there has to be more to life than this...*

A shadow passed across the dipping sun, darkening the extravagant pink and gold evening. Walking across the lawn in search of Scarlet, Lily was aware of a throbbing in her head; a steady, rhythmic pulsing, like a second heartbeat, which only seemed to intensify her edginess.

This year the theme of the party was Myths and Legends, and as the sun cast long shadows across the grass silken-clad girls with elaborate, shimmering fairy wings were mingling with Greek gods and screen icons. Several large marquees stood around the fringes of the lawn, with a space in the centre where, according to Scarlet, a troop of semi-naked stunt riders were going to perform later.

On unicorns, apparently.

A warm breeze was stirring the leaves of the stately horse chestnut trees, making them bend and sigh. By this time tomorrow she would be half a world away in the arid heart of Africa, and all of this would seem more like a dream than ever, if that were possible. Perhaps it was normal to feel like this just before a trip like the one she was about to embark on? She was branching out from the safe confines of the shallow, superficial life and plunging straight into the depths of a world that until now she had only read about in the papers and seen on TV news reports. Being nervous was probably completely understandable. Except that nervous didn't quite describe the feeling she had…

Restless.

The word flashed into her head from nowhere, echoing round it, amplified by the throbbing that was growing louder all the time. She tipped her head back, suddenly aware that the evening air held a kind of tension; a pulsing energy that resonated inside her, filling her with a sense of anticipation. A helicopter was suspended high above and, mesmerised, she watched its blades slicing through the soft apricot sky as it circled like some dark, powerful predator.

Suddenly she jumped as the mobile phone she was clutching tightly in her hand rang, breaking the spell. She answered quickly, pressing it tightly to her ear so that the shrieks of laughter and the sporadic bursts of ear-splitting music from the rock band that was tuning up in the marquee couldn't be heard on the other end of the line by the director of the African children's charity with which she was going to be working.

'Yes, fine, thank you, Jack. All ready for tomorrow, I think….'

The noise persisted, all but drowning out Jack Davidson's voice, and Lily walked quickly across the lawn away from the party in the hope of finding somewhere quiet to talk.

'Yes, I'm still here…' she said loudly. 'Sorry, it's a bad line.'

She kept her head down, focusing all her attention on the voice in her ear. Jack was running through the itinerary for the trip, and the words 'orphanage' and 'feeding station' seemed utterly incongruous in her present luxurious surroundings. She kept walking, rounding the corner of the castle with its massive stone turret and heading out across the open ground beyond. She had left behind the lush greenness of the formal gardens and was now crossing an area of rough, parched grass behind the castle. The sounds of the party were muted here, but the noise of the helicopter blades was getting louder, pulsing insistently through the honeyed afternoon, whipping up the heavy air until Lily felt as if she were standing in the eye of the storm.

High above, Tristan Romero smiled as he watched her.

The reason he hadn't seen her earlier, he realised, was that her pale golden colouring had made her melt perfectly into the drought bleached grass of the field. She was like a goddess of the harvest, he thought with a stab of curiosity as he hovered above her. She was wearing some kind of delicate crown of golden leaves on her head, but this didn't stop her long, wheat-coloured hair rippling out in heavy streamers in the wind from the rotor blades. She stood still, struggling to hold down her dress as it billowed up around her, but her efforts were hampered by the fact that she was holding a mobile phone to her ear with one hand and a glass of champagne in the other, and simultaneously trying to control her wind-blown hair.

He came down just in front of her and couldn't resist keeping the blades going for a minute longer than was necessary, so he could enjoy the delicious spectacle of her long, long brown legs beneath the flyaway dress, which was being flattened against the most incredible body.

There was something familiar about her, he thought as he pulled off his headset and jumped down from the cabin. In the sudden stillness she had shaken back her heavy hair and as he walked towards her he got a proper look at her face. He wondered whether he'd slept with her before.

No. With a body like that he would almost certainly have remembered. She was tall, but there was a slow grace in her movements that told him that bedding her would be an unforgettable experience. Tristan felt desire uncurl somewhere low down in his exhausted body. She was still on the phone, her head bent, clearly totally preoccupied with the conversation she was having. As he got closer he heard her say, 'Yes, yes, don't worry, I know it's important, but I'm writing it all down. I've got all the details here in front of me.'

A beautiful girl with an outrageous disregard for the truth.

How intriguing, he thought as she finished her conversation and looked up at him.

He felt a small shock jolt through his body, as if he had just touched a live wire. Against the golden tones of her hair and skin and dress, her eyes were a cool, clear silver; the colour of the mist that hung over the lake first thing in the morning.

'Eight-thirty,' she said out loud. Her voice was slightly breathless, and she was looking straight at him, but almost as if she weren't seeing him. 'Eight-thirty, tomorrow morning. Heathrow Terminal One.'

He smiled, quirking an eyebrow as he carried on walking towards her. 'I'll remind you when we wake up,' he said dryly.

It was a joke. A throwaway remark. He had made it without even intending to stop walking, but the moment the words left his lips two things happened.

Firstly, he heard it: the quiet cicada whirr of a camera shutter, and from the corner of his eye caught the glint of a lens in the shadow of the trees. And secondly, he saw the instantaneous darkening of those extraordinary silver eyes.

Tristan Romero had many skills. Heading up the list had to be seducing women and manipulating the press. He didn't even have to think about it. Before she could utter a single word of protest he had put his hand around her waist and was pulling her towards him.

The first thing she had noticed about him was his eyes.

His dark hair was cut close into his perfect neck, a couple of days of stubble emphasised sculpted cheekbones and his skin was tanned to a deep, even gold that made the blue of his eyes seem almost shocking. Looking up into them, desperately trying to imprint on her memory the instructions she'd just been given for meeting the rest of the African expedition tomorrow, Lily felt her throat tighten as sharply as if someone had wrapped a cord around her neck and pulled it. Hard.

Blue.

Blue you could float in.

Drown in.

She'd spoken out loud because she knew that all the information that she'd just been given was in danger of evaporating from her brain like water hitting hot stone. His answering remark was clearly a joke, but her body didn't seem to get the humour. The world stopped and time vanished into a vortex of cinematic, freeze-frame intimacy as the blueness pulled her down. In the deep underwater world of his eyes everything slowed. Lily could hear nothing but the drumming of her pulse in her ears, feel nothing but the bloom of heat beneath the surface of her skin, the prickle of awareness low down in her pelvis.

And then he'd pulled her against him and she wasn't drowning any more. She was *burning*. His kiss was pure magic. Firm, expert, and shockingly tender. Lily felt as if the sinking sun had slipped from the flame-streaked sky and set the world on fire, and that she were standing in the midst of the leaping flames with no desire to be rescued. His arm was around her waist, his hand resting in the small of her back. Lily felt herself arching helplessly towards him, her hands—still holding the phone and the champagne glass—hanging uselessly by her sides as her lips opened for him and the darkness behind her closed eyes glittered and glowed with blistering lust.

'He's here!'

It was just a distant shout, but suddenly he was lifting his head, pulling away slightly so that his blue eyes met hers. For a second Lily caught a look that was almost like despair in their depths, but then it was gone and he was letting her go.

Dazedly she turned round. From the direction of the party Scarlet and Tom were walking towards them, hand in hand, and behind them came a drift of girls dressed as fairies and mermaids and wood nymphs in shimmering silks and floaty chiffons.

'Finally!' Tom shouted, his kind face breaking into a grin as he walked up to the man who had just fallen out of the sky like some avenging angel and kissed her to within an inch of her life. With his pale, romantic English looks Tom looked absurdly at home in his St George costume, and oddly pure and noble next to the dangerous glamour of the beautiful stranger. 'I see you've already met Lily,' he said easily.

'*Lily…*' The devastatingly sexy mouth that moments ago had been caressing hers now twisted into an ironic, mocking smile as that blue gaze swept over her, taking in the coronet of golden laurel leaves in her hair and the Grecian pleated silk dress. 'That makes it easier. I wasn't sure if you were meant to be Helen of Troy or Demeter, goddess of the harvest.'

Lily felt the colour flood her cheeks. The dress was one she had worn in a shoot a couple of years ago when the Gladiator look had been at its peak. Suddenly she wished she'd taken the time to plan something a bit more interesting, like Scarlet, who was stunning in a little black dress and diamonds as Coco Chanel.

'I was kind of thinking Helen of Troy…' she said awkwardly, not meeting his eye.

'Of course. The face that launched a thousand products. You're the girl from the perfume advertisements?'

Lily nodded, jumping like a startled deer as he reached out and took hold of her wrist, raising it slowly. Her first thought was that he was going to kiss her hand, but he turned it palm upwards and his thumb brushed the blue-veined skin of her wrist. Then he bent his head and breathed in.

'Every time I see one of those adverts I wonder if the perfume smells as good as you make it look,' he said thoughtfully. 'But I never actually imagined it would be possible.'

His voice seemed to reach down inside her and caress her in places she'd never been touched before. His English was perfect, but the Spanish accent ran through it like wine through water. Lily had to force herself to focus on his words. To reply to them.

'I'm not wearing it,' she stammered. 'Not tonight. I'm not wearing anything.'

Oh God. Had she really said that?

'Really?' His mouth curved into a smile that would have

melted ice caps, and yet didn't quite manage to warm those cool
blue eyes. 'What a very appealing image that conjures up.'

For a heartbeat he looked at her, and then he turned away.

And that was how he did it, Lily thought as heat and liquid
excitement cascaded through her, drenching her body from
within while her logical mind switched off and shut down.
Whoever he was, he had a way of drawing you in with one
hand and then slamming the door in your face with the other.
It wasn't nice, but, God, was it effective. She felt disorientated,
unhinged by what had happened, as if he had kidnapped and
brainwashed her, and then thrust her back out into ordinary
life.

Lily was aware of Scarlet desperately trying to catch her eye,
but then Tom pulled her forward and was saying, with mock for-
mality, 'Scarlet, I want you to meet Tristan Romero de Losada;
Montalvo, Marqués of Montesa, and my oldest friend.'

Lily's heart gave a violent jolt, as if electrical pads had just
been pressed to her chest.

Tristan Romero de Losada Montalvo?

Oh, God. How could she not have recognised him?

But the truth was that none of the grainy, long-lens photographs in the tabloids or close-up red-carpet shots in the glossy
magazines could have prepared her for the impact of seeing the
Marqués of Montesa in the bronzed and beautiful flesh.

Introductions over, Scarlet came over to her and Lily seized
her arm and dragged her a little way away, back towards the
castle and the rest of the party.

'Tom's *best friend* is Tristan Romero de Losada? From the
uber-aristocratic Spanish banking family?'

Scarlet looked amused. 'That's right. They've been best
friends even longer than we have, since they were locked up
together in some grim Dickensian prep school as little boys.'

Lily's head was spinning. The lingering pleasure from his
kiss mixed with shock and shame that she could have been so

easily taken in. 'But Tom's so nice,' she faltered, 'and he's… he's…*wicked*.'

'Lil-y,' said Scarlet reproachfully. 'You should know better than most not to believe everything you read in the papers—or at least to understand that it's never the entire story. Tom won't hear a word against him—apparently Tristan practically saved his life on more than one occasion when Tom was bullied at school. Anyway,' she said, turning to Lily with a speculative look, 'how come you seem to know so much about him? Since you'd rather read Nietzsche in the original than a tabloid newspaper, you seem very well informed.'

'Everyone knows about him,' Lily muttered darkly as they walked back towards the castle. 'You don't even have to read the tabloids. The broadsheets and the financial pages mention the Romero name pretty regularly too, you know.' Most reporters were torn between disapproval and awe at the breathtaking ruthlessness that had ensured that the Romero bank had ridden out all the economic storms of modern times and remained one of the most significant players in global finance, and the Romero family one of the richest and most powerful in the world.

'Anyway,' she said, aware that she sounded like a sulky child, but unable to stop herself, 'what's he come as? James Bond? He's hardly a myth or a legend.'

'Darling, he hasn't come as anything. He's the one person for whom Tom makes an exception to the fancy dress rule. He's come as himself—legendary Euro Playboy, mythical sex god. He'll have left some party on a yacht in Marbella or the bed of some raving beauty in a chateau in the Loire and come straight here.' She gave a gasp of laughter, which she quickly stifled, and leaned closer to Lily's ear. 'In something of a hurry, I'd say. Check out his shirt. It's buttoned up all wrong.'

Glancing backwards, Lily's eyes went automatically to his chest. Scarlet was right. Beneath the dark, slightly crumpled jacket of his perfectly tailored suit, his white shirt was untucked, the collar open, lopsided, showing an expanse of deep golden flesh and one sculpted collarbone.

She wasn't sure which was worse: the instant rush of hot indignant anger that the kiss that had turned her inside out with longing had been given so casually, so randomly by a man whose body was barely cold from another woman's bed.

Or the low down ache of desire, and the shameful knowledge that she didn't care. That she just wanted to kiss him again.

'Everything OK?' said Tom out of the corner of his mouth. They had walked back across the field to the party and were now striding across the lawn towards the marquee where the bar was.

Tristan gave a curt nod. 'Sorry I'm late. I couldn't get away.'

'Not a problem. For me, anyway, although your extensive collection of female hangers-on have been getting increasingly restless. I was running out of answers for where you could be.'

'A house party in St Tropez is the official story.'

Tom threw him a swift grin. 'It must have been some party. Perhaps you'd better do your shirt up properly, old friend, or we might have a riot on our hands.'

Tristan glanced down with a grimace. Dressing quickly when he'd landed his plane at the nearby airfield, he'd been so tired he'd hardly been able to see straight. Hardly the ideal circumstances to get ready for what was always dubbed the social event of the year. The mild air pulsed with music from one of the marquees around the lawn, an insistent reminder that yet another sleepless night lay ahead of him.

'So that's the official story,' said Tom soberly, 'but what's the truth?'

'Khazakismir,' Tristan replied tonelessly, looking straight ahead and unbuttoning his shirt as they walked across the lawn towards the tented bar.

Tom winced at the name. 'I hoped you weren't going to say that. News coverage here has been patchy, but I gather things are pretty grim?'

The name of the small province in a remote corner of Eastern Europe had become synonymous with despair and violence in the course of a decade-long war, the original purpose of which no one could remember any more. Power rested in the blood-stained hands of a corrupt military government and a few drugs barons, who quashed any sign of civil unrest quickly and ruthlessly. Reports had filtered through in the last week of a whole village being laid to waste.

'You could say that.' A door in Tristan's mind swung open, letting the images flood back into his head for a moment before he mentally slammed it shut again. 'One of our drivers was caught up in it. His family were killed—everyone apart from his sister, who's pregnant.' His mouth quirked into a bitter smile. 'It seems that the military were keen to make use of the brand new cache of weaponry they have courtesy of funds from the Romero bank.'

Pausing at the entrance to the marquee, Tom laid a hand on his arm.

'Are you OK?'

'Fine,' he said tersely. 'You know me. I don't get involved in the humanitarian side. I'm just there to help out with practicalities. Redress the balance.'

He didn't meet Tom's eyes as he spoke, looking instead over his shoulder and into the distance, where the lake lay in its hollow of shadows, the tower in the centre wreathed in mist. A muscle flickered in his jaw.

'Anything I can do?' Tom said quietly.

Tristan flashed a brief, ironic smile as they moved into the damp, alcohol-scented warmth of the marquee. 'I haven't been seen anywhere for a while, so I could do with giving the press their pound of flesh. If any word got out tying me to activities over there it would be a security nightmare.'

Tom's smile didn't waver as he shouldered his way through to the bar, nodding a welcome to his guests. Speaking quietly, he said, 'That's easily arranged. The usual tame photographers are here, the society event ones who have progressed slightly further up the evolutionary scale from the paparazzi, but if you pick someone high profile and enjoy a little bit of public affection, I'm sure they'll regress into mindless savages who'll sell your picture to every glossy magazine and sleazy gossip rag by Monday morning.' He took two glasses from the tray on the bar and handed one to Tristan. 'Cheers, old chap. So—who's it going to be?'

'Lily.' Tristan tossed back the dark coloured liquid in the shot glass, feeling it burning a path down his throat as he watched Tom's open face fall. He was gauging his reaction before admitting what had already happened. It wasn't positive.

'No. No way. Not a good idea.'

'Why not? She's high profile.' And beautiful, there was no doubt about that. Even Tristan, tired and jaded, had been jolted by it, which had surprised him. It was more than that, though. For a moment back there when she was in his arms he had found himself looking into her slanting, silvery grey eyes and felt almost...

Almost human?

'She's also Scarlet's best friend,' Tom said firmly. 'You screw her up—which let's face it, you certainly will—and you screw things up for me.'

'Why would I screw her up?' Tristan picked up another shot glass and looked restlessly around. 'She's a model, Tom; hard as nails and, judging from what I just saw, not really all there. She'll end up with something shiny and expensive from Cartier, and a whole raft of publicity, and I'll feed the press appetite to portray me as a pointless playboy and throw them off the scent. Everyone's happy.'

Tom looked worried. 'I don't think she's like that.'

'You're too nice, Tom, my friend,' Tristan said grimly, draining his glass. 'They're all like that.'

CHAPTER TWO

As TWILIGHT fell it brought with it a kind of enchantment. Paper lanterns glowed palely in the trees and the scattering of diamond stars that glittered in the purple heavens looked as if they'd been placed there purely for the delight of the guests.

Lily wouldn't have been surprised. Nothing was impossible here tonight.

Earlier, as waiters had circulated with cool green cocktails that tasted of melons and champagne, masked girls dressed as dryads and wood nymphs had appeared from the shadowy trees that fringed the lawn on white horses, with delicate, spiralling unicorn's horns on their foreheads. To the haunting strains of a full orchestra headed by a stunning girl playing an electric violin they had performed a display of equestrian dance, weaving around each other, making the horses rear and pirouette, until Lily wasn't sure if she was dreaming. Once, through the writhing, stamping figures of the unicorns, she found herself staring straight into the eyes of Tristan, standing opposite, his shirt half unbuttoned and his arm around a well-known young Hollywood actress dressed as Pocahontas. A shock, like a small electrocution, sizzled through her.

The next time she looked he was gone.

She had hardly touched her cocktail. She didn't need to. Already she felt heavy and languid with tiredness, but beneath that there was an edge of restlessness, a throbbing pulse of desire and impatience and wild longing that alcohol would only exacerbate. The riding display finished and the unicorns melted back into the darkness that had gathered beneath the trees. Lily turned to say something to Scarlet, but she had moved away slightly and was standing with Tom. His arms were looped around her waist and as Lily watched he pulled her into him and spoke into her ear.

Lily felt a beat of pain, of anguish, deep inside her chest and turned away.

She and Scarlet had been a team for so long. All through school at a fairly rough comprehensive in Brighton it had been the two of them—united by both being tall, skinny and teased for it—until the day when Maggie Mason had spotted them shopping together in The Lanes and invited them both up to London for an interview at her famous modelling agency. Lily had been so set on going to university, if it hadn't been for Scarlet there was no way she would have even taken Maggie's card. But they had been in it together, two halves of the same whole—as different as it was possible to be. But always together.

Which was, she told herself firmly, why she was so pleased for Scarlet. Tom was lovely, and when she thought of some of the unsuitable men that her friend could have fallen in love with…

Tristan Romero de Losada Montalvo, for example.

The violinist was playing solo now, a gentle, haunting melody that echoed across the mist-shrouded fields and gentle hills enfolding the castle. Another horse cantered into the ring, this time with the most fantastic pair of wings attached to its saddle. A murmur of delight ran around the crowd, which quickly turned to a gasp of surprise as the scantily clad girl rider opened the lid of the basket she carried.

There was a flurry of feathers, a whispered beat of wings and a flock of white doves spiralled upwards into the sky. In the smudged violet light their wings were almost luminescent. For a moment they seemed to hang motionless in the air, as if uncertain what to do with their unexpected freedom, and out of the corner of her eye Lily caught a movement in the crowd opposite. She turned her head, and was just in time to see a man in a Robin Hood costume raise his bow and arrow and take a shot.

A macho jeer went up from the group around him as one of the doves faltered, losing height for a minute in a ragged tumble of feathers. Lily could see the arrow, hanging tenuously from the bird's side, seeming to drag it downwards. Miraculously the bird didn't fall but, with an odd, lopsided flapping, flew down towards the lake.

Rage exploded inside her. The display was over and the crowd began to drift away towards the next entertainment, but Lily began to run, down the sloping lawn to the water. The grass was cool and damp beneath her bare feet and as she got near the lake the ground grew softer. Heart hammering, she pushed her way through the thick tangle of undergrowth and looked around, across the glassy surface of the water to the island in its centre.

The ruined walls of the stone tower were dark against the faded lilac sky behind, but in the stillness she could hear the agitated beating of wings. Doves rose from the broken ramparts at the top, and she strained her eyes into the gloom to see if the injured one was amongst them. What if the arrow was still there, lodged in the bird's flesh?

Her eyes stung and frustration drummed in her head as she peered up into the nebulous sky, but it was impossible to make anything out clearly. With a gasp of exasperation she was just about to turn back when she noticed a wooden walkway at the back of the tower leading across the stretch of water to the island. Hurrying round, she felt the brambles snag at the hem of her dress and the damp grass cling to her legs. The walkway was narrow, the boards old and very smooth, but stepping tentatively onto them Lily could feel that it was sturdily made.

From across the lawn she could hear more yells of hilarity above the bass beat of the music as the party escalated, which only strengthened her resolve and refuelled her fury. The sound of the doves at the top of the tower was a soft murmur, but it was comforting as she stepped onto the dark island.

In spite of the warmth of the evening she shivered. Everything was inky, insubstantial; layers of grey that melted into each other until it was impossible to say what was real and what was shadow. The air was heavy with the scent of roses and through the indigo dusk Lily could see their pale globes clustered around a small door in the tower.

Her heart was knocking so violently against her ribs that she could feel it shaking her whole body as she went towards the door. Hesitantly, almost hoping that it would be locked, she put her hand against the blistered wood.

It sprang open, without her even pushing. Lily gasped; a sharp indrawn breath of pure fear as a figure appeared in the doorway, white shirt ghostly in the opaque light. She leapt backwards, pressing her hand to her mouth, choking with fear as the man reached out and caught her, pulling her back towards him.

'Helen of Troy.' The voice was very deep, very scathing, very Spanish. He gave her a little shake. 'You followed me, I suppose?'

Lily's heart was almost beating out of her chest, but the arrogance of his words penetrated her shocked haze. '*No!* I came to look for a bird…an injured dove. Some…*idiot* with a bow and arrow took a shot at it when they were released and it flew in this direction. When I came to look for it I saw that they'd flown up to the roof of the tower, but I didn't know that you were here—' She stopped suddenly, as the most likely explanation for Tristan Romero to be discovered on a secluded island in the middle of a party popped into her horrified mind, and then tried to take a hasty step backwards. 'Sorry. I'll go.'

His hand tightened around her arm. 'No. Don't let me stop your mission of mercy,' he drawled. 'There's a dovecote on the roof. Go up and look for it.'

She hesitated, remembering the Pocahontas girl. 'Are you here alone?'

'Yes.' Against his white shirt his skin looked very dark, and the hollows beneath his hard cheekbones were inky. Apart from that it was impossible to see his face in any detail, but his voice was like sandpaper and when he laughed there was no humour in it. 'I take it Tom's warned you off. Perhaps you'd prefer to come back with a chaperone?'

His fingers were still circling her wrist. She could feel her rapid pulse beating against his thumb. 'Don't be ridiculous,' she said, with a brave attempt at scorn. 'I just didn't want to *interrupt* anything, that's all. Now, if you'd like to tell me where to go?'

He let go of her, stepping back into the shadows with a sweep of his arm. 'Up to the top of the stairs.'

Inside the tower the air was chill and damp. A stone staircase spiralled above them, and Lily's bare feet made no sound on the ice cold stone as she began to climb up. The staircase opened onto a small landing halfway up, where a narrow, arrow-slit window spilled soft light onto a closed door. Lily stopped outside the door, but Tristan walked past her, leading the way up another twisting staircase.

At the top he pushed open another door and stood back to let her through first. Lily stepped out and turned around slowly, letting out a low exhalation of awe as she did so.

From below it looked as if the tower were half ruined, the stone walls crumbling and uneven, but now she could see that this was a deliberate illusion. The platform she now stood on was paved with smooth stone flags, and all around the insides of the thick stone walls that looked so dilapidated from the other side of the lake were recessed ledges where birds could nest. But this hardly made an impression. It was the view that stole her breath. Over the lowest part of the wall she could see the pink stained sky beyond the trees that fringed the far side of the lake. At the front of the tower the wall was higher, but a narrow gothic-style arched window framed a view over the lake to the gardens and the castle and the fields beyond, making it possible to look out without being observed. Lily walked over to it.

'It's amazing. I thought this was a ruin; an empty shell.'

'That's the idea,' said Tristan from the doorway. 'It was commissioned by one of Tom's more inventive ancestors, and intended to appear decorative but functionless. In reality it's an incredibly cleverly designed gambling den. Where you're standing now is a lookout post, so that anyone approaching could be seen long before they had any chance of getting here.'

Lily shook her head and laughed softly, tilting her head back and looking up at the violet velvet sky, feeling suddenly light and breathless. Tristan levered himself away from the low doorframe where he'd been leaning, and came slowly towards her.

Her pulse quickened, and she felt the laughter die on her lips as electricity crackled through her. In the hazy half-light his eyes were dark blue, his face grave, and she sensed again that weary despair she had glimpsed in him earlier. Suddenly she found it impossible to reconcile this achingly beautiful man who wore sadness like an invisible cloak with the sybaritic playboy whose libertine lifestyle so fascinated the gutter press.

'You're right.'

Lily gave a small, startled gasp, wondering how he'd managed to read her mind, but then he raised one hand, gesturing to a recess in the wall beside her.

'The injured dove,' he said tonelessly. 'There it is.'

'Oh…' She frowned, stooping down and letting her hair fall across her face as she felt heat spread upwards. The bird was huddled in the back of the nesting recess, its wing held up awkwardly. The white feathers were stained with crimson at the place where the wing joined the body. 'Poor thing…' Lily crooned gently. 'Poor, poor thing…'

Tristan felt his throat tighten inexplicably. Her voice was filled with a tenderness that seemed to slip right past his iron defences and go straight into the battered, shell-shocked heart of him.

Usually he slipped between lives with the insouciant agility of an alley cat, letting the doors between the two halves of his world swing tightly shut behind him. But tonight—*Dios*—tonight he was finding it hard to leave it all behind. The raucous revelry of the party had grated on his frayed nerves like salt in an open wound, which was why he'd had to get away. But this…

This gentle compassion was almost worse. Because it was harder to withstand.

'I think its wing is broken,' Lily said softly. 'What can we do?'

He looked out over the lawn to the glittering lights of the party. 'Nothing,' he said, hearing the harshness in his voice. 'If that's the case it would be best to end its suffering quickly and kill it now.'

'No!' Her response was instantaneous and fierce. She stood up, placing herself between him and the bird, almost as if she were afraid he was going to grab it and wring its neck in front of her.

'You couldn't. You wouldn't…'

'Why not?' he said brutally as images of the place he had been earlier flashed into his head with jagged, strobe-lit insistence. This was just a bird, for God's sake. An injured bird; a pity, not a tragedy. 'Why not end its suffering?'

'Because you don't have the right to play God like that,' she said quietly. 'None of us do.'

Standing in the last light of the fading day, she looked remote and almost mystically beautiful. Not of this world. What did she know about suffering? He could feel the pulse beating loudly in his ears, but her words cut through it, exploding inside his head. *No?* he wanted to say. *Then who will? It's not power that makes men behave like God, but desperation.*

He turned away abruptly, walking back towards the door to the stairs. 'It's not about having the right,' he said bleakly. 'It's about having the guts.'

'Wait!'

He heard her come down after him, and the blue twilight darkened as she shut the door at the top of the stairs again. Tristan stopped on the landing, his shoulders against the closed door, and watched her come down the stairs, melting out of the shadows like something from a dream.

Slowly she came down the last couple of steps and stood in front of him, shaking her head. 'I don't,' she said in a low voice. 'I don't have the guts to kill it. What shall I do?'

He shrugged. 'Sometimes you just have to accept that there's nothing you can do.'

'But that's—'

'Life,' he said flatly. 'That's—'

But he didn't finish, because at that moment the dusk was shattered by two loud explosions that detonated a chain of nightmarish images and sent an instant tide of adrenaline crashing through him. He saw her start violently, her head snapping round to the window, her eyes wide with shock. Pure instinct took over. Without thinking he reached for her, pulling her into his body, against his crashing heart as he shouldered open the door behind him and dragged her into the room beyond.

The next moment the sky beyond the two tall, arched Gothic windows was lit up with showers of glittering stars.

Fireworks. It was fireworks. Not bombs and mortars. Relief hit him, followed a heartbeat later by another sensation; less welcome, but every bit as powerful as he became aware of the feel of her breasts beneath the silk of her dress, crushed against his chest. As another volley of blasts split the sky she pulled away from him, laughing shakily.

And then she looked around her at the hexagonal room, with its pale grey walls and its arched windows and the bed with the carved wooden posts at its centre, and suddenly she wasn't laughing any more.

'Yours?' she whispered.

He nodded briefly. Over the years he'd lent Tom more money than either of them bothered to keep track of. The tower was a token return for his investment. 'It's where I come when I want to be alone.'

Their gazes locked. Time hitched, hanging suspended. Her full lips were parted, her breathing was rapid and her grey eyes shone with shimmering colour from the fireworks that exploded above them. Then she blinked and looked away.

'Oh. I see, I'm sorry—I'll go.'

She moved towards the door, but he got there first, slamming it shut and standing with his shoulders against it.

'Tonight I don't want to be alone.'

CHAPTER THREE

ADRENALINE was pulsing through Tristan, making the beat of his heart hard and painful. It vibrated through his whole body as the explosions continued outside—audacious reminders of the things he had travelled around half the world to forget.

In the grainy, blurred light Lily's luminous beauty had an ethereal quality. Her eyes were still fixed on his, and as he gazed into them he felt the panic recede a little, washed away by the warm, anaesthetising tide of desire. Rationality slipped away, like sand through his fingers. For a moment he battled to hold onto it, to anchor himself back in the world of reason, but then she moved forward so she was standing right in front of him and he could see the spiked shadows cast by her lashes on the high arc of her cheekbone and feel the whispering sigh of her breath on his skin as she exhaled shakily.

'I don't want to be alone, either,' she said in a low voice. 'But I don't want to go back to the party.'

Slowly, almost reluctantly, he reached out and touched the gleaming curve of her bare shoulder with his fingertip. He felt her jerk slightly beneath his touch, as if it had burned her, and an answering jolt of sharp, clenching desire shot through him.

With deliberate slowness he bent his head, inhaling her scent as he brought his lips down to her shoulder. 'You don't like parties?'

'I don't like crowds. I prefer...' she breathed, then gave a soft, shivering gasp as his mouth brushed her skin '…privacy. I don't like being looked at.'

'You're in the wrong job,' Tristan said dryly.

'Tell me about it.'

There was a wistful ache in her voice that made him lift his head and look into her face. For a fleeting moment he glimpsed the bleakness there, but then she was tilting her head up to his, her lips parting as they rose to meet his, and the questions that were forming in his head dissolved like snow in summer.

He didn't want to know anyway. He didn't want to *talk* to her, for pity's sake. This was purely physical.

Not emotional.

Never emotional.

Her hands came up to cup his head, her fingers sliding into his hair, pulling him down, harder, deeper. He sensed a hunger in her that matched his own. The silk dress hung loosely from her shoulders and he knew that simply slipping the narrow, gathered straps downwards would make it fall to the floor, but he forced himself to wait, to take it slowly, to suppress the naked savagery of his need.

Above all, *this* was why he had come. Tom and the press were just convenient excuses.

This was his salvation, his purifying baptismal fire. This was where he lost himself, purged himself of all the images from the last week that haunted him whenever he closed his eyes. It didn't matter whose body he lost himself in, whose lips he was kissing. It meant nothing. It was simply a means to an end.

A way of remembering the joy of being alive, the pleasures of the flesh.

A way of forgetting.

Lily pulled away, taking a deep, gasping breath of air, trying to steady herself against the swelling tide of pure desire that threatened to sweep her away. The light was fading quickly now; the sky beyond the arched windows was the soft, lush purple of clematis petals and the walls of the tower room had melted into it, making it feel as if they'd been cut adrift from reality and were floating far out at sea. Tristan's hands rested on her shoulders, his thumbs beneath her jaw, stopping her from dropping her head, ducking away from meeting his gaze. In a world of smudged inky shades of blue and mauve his eyes were as deep and dark as a tropical ocean.

'I have to warn you,' he said roughly, 'this is just tonight. One night. No strings, no commitment, no happy ever after. Is that what you want?'

His honesty made her breath catch. No promises, no lies. Somewhere, distantly, she was aware of pain, of disappointment, but it was numbed by the dizzying lust that circulated through her body like a drug. In the morning she was leaving for Africa—a different world, a new direction in her life. Tonight stood alone; a bridge between the old and the new. There were no rules, only the imperatives of the moment. Of forgetting about tomorrow, and giving herself something to remember when it came.

'Yes,' she whispered, lifting her hands to the neck of his shirt, sliding them beneath the open collar. 'Just tonight.'

Outside another explosion ripped the sky apart with a shower of pink stars and she felt him flinch slightly. Carefully she began to undo the buttons of his shirt. There was nothing hurried about her movements, though her hands shook a little with the effort of keeping them steady, of reining back the powerful need that was building within her. He stood completely still as caressingly she trailed the backs of her fingers down the strip of lean, well-muscled flesh that was revealed by his unbuttoned shirt, and the only evidence of his desire was the quickening thud of his heart.

Her hand moved downwards, skimming over the buckle of his belt.

Not the only evidence… She felt his whole body tense as her palm brushed the hardness of his arousal beneath his clothes. For a second his head tipped back, as if he was in pain, but then he seemed to gather himself, and as his hands gripped her shoulders Lily couldn't tell whether he was taking control or abandoning it.

The bed was as pale and cool as a lunar landscape in the mystical blue twilight. Tristan's hands slipped down her arms, making her shiver, and then he was taking her hands in his and drawing her towards it. She wasn't aware of the ground beneath her feet any more. Stars, brighter even than the ones lighting up the washed out sky outside, filled her head, gold and glittering as, very gently, he pushed one strap of her dress down over her shoulder and stroked a circle of bliss over the skin he had exposed.

Lily bit her lip to stop herself crying out into the thick silence. With maddening, excruciating slowness Tristan turned his attention to the other shoulder. In the fading light his face bore an expression of detached intensity, which made tongues of fire leap along her nerves, burning pathways into the hungry, molten core of her. With a care that was almost abstracted he took the pleated silk between his fingers, holding it for a second before sliding it off her shoulder.

The dress slithered to the floor like a curtain coming down, and Lily stood before him, naked apart from a pair of tiny silk knickers.

She was almost too beautiful, Tristan thought with an edge of despair. Too perfect.

As she stood there, the muted evening folding around her like veils of blue voile, softening the planes and angles of her impossibly slender body and silvering the coronet of leaves in her hair, she looked like some remote and untouchable figure from ancient mythology. With careful restraint he reached out and took her waist between his hands, stroking his thumbs upwards to the small, exquisite breasts.

'Selene...' he murmured, and her head jerked back, her eyes filled with shock and hurt, but he felt the convulsive tremor that shook her as his palms brushed her hardened nipples and she didn't try to move away.

'No!' she said harshly, raggedly. 'That's not my name. I'm Lily...'

Tristan laughed softly. Her misplaced insecurity touched him. As if anyone would forget her name. 'I know that.' He bent his head, pressing his lips to the pale skin below her collarbone, unhurriedly moving downwards. 'Earlier I thought you were a golden Demeter, but now you look like Selene, the goddess of the moon.'

She closed her eyes and buried her shy smile in the silk of his hair. 'Tell me about her.'

'She fell in love with a mortal—a handsome shepherd boy called Endymion—and she couldn't bear the thought of ever being separated from him.' Tristan's mouth hovered for a second over the tight bud of her nipple, the warmth of his breath caressing the quivering, darkened flesh until he felt his own desire pounding at the barriers of his self-control. 'So she asked Zeus to grant him eternal sleep, so that he would never die and never grow older. Every night she used to go and lie with him.'

He straightened up and looked at her. Her eyes were incandescent with unconcealed need but laughter gleamed in their depths as she raised herself up onto her tiptoes to kiss him again.

'You seem to be on first name terms with all the A-list goddesses,' she said softly against his mouth. 'Either you have friends in very high places or a degree in Classics.'

He pulled away sharply, dipping his head downwards so she couldn't see his face. 'Neither,' he said tonelessly. 'I have *half* a degree in Classics.'

'You gave it up?'

'Yes. I dropped out.' His voice was soft, but he couldn't quite keep the bitterness from it as he pressed his mouth against her scented skin and pushed away the thoughts of the life he should have had. He heard her gasp as he ran the tip of his tongue around the rosy halo of her nipple and he felt her whole body momentarily convulse against him as he took her deeper into his mouth, sucking, kissing, losing himself in her.

Her arms tightened around his neck, her breath in his ear was a soft siren song of want. The familiar room, his refuge, his private sanctuary, blurred and blackened as the blood pounded in his head, a primitive, insistent rhythm, drowning out everything else but the miracle of her cool, creamy flesh on his tongue.

Sense left him. His brain—exhausted, jaded, cynical—crashed, and the jagged pattern of his constant, tormented thoughts levelled out into a flat line of submission while his body and his senses took over. Her hands were on his belt, working swiftly, deftly at the buckle, then pushing his trousers downwards, his underwear too, and together they sank down onto the bed, their mouths not leaving each other, their hands not pausing in their urgent, hungry exploration. Dimly Tristan was aware that his shirt still hung loose and unbuttoned from his shoulders, but he was too far gone to stop and take it off.

He was too far gone for anything. The awfulness of the last few days, the constant, grinding stress, the relentless horror that pushed at the steel barriers he placed around his mind had suddenly gone, sucked into the vortex of physical need, of blissful annihilation. It was as if some inbuilt survival mechanism had clicked into place inside him, finally shutting off the maddening need to think and plan and stay rigidly in control...

Did she sense this as she pushed him gently back onto the moonlit bed, and rose above him? Her flawless skin was bleached to ghostly whiteness, intensifying the dark glitter of her eyes and the crimson of her kiss-bruised mouth as she dipped her head and slid down his thighs, parting her glistening lips and...

The outside world slipped from focus. Even the machine-gun snap of the fireworks faded to a dull crackle. There was nothing beyond the sensation of her soft mouth on his burning, swollen flesh, the feathery caress of her hair brushing his skin as she bent over him. Opening his eyes, looking down, he could see the pale arc of her back. In his dazzled head her shoulder blades looked like angel's wings.

Dios... Dios mio...

He was on the edge, on the brink of oblivion, holding on by his fingernails, but he wouldn't allow himself to let go and hurtle through the secret darkness to his own bliss. Sitting up, he caught hold of her and, sliding his hands into her hair, pulled her head up.

'My turn now.'

Meeting his eyes through the blue gloom Lily was instantly flooded with slippery heat. Though his face was tense and set, they were black and liquid with arousal. Wordlessly she let him pull her towards him, so that they were facing each other on the moon-drenched bed. One hand was in her hair, his strong fingers slowly massaging her scalp, sending shivering electrical impulses down through her entire body. The other remained at his side as he looked at her.

He simply *looked*...

Lily Alexander was used to being looked at. It was her job. Her life. It made her feel many things...resentful, jaded, uncomfortable, contemptuous... Never like this before. Never as if she were burning from the inside, as if fire were spreading from the cradle of her pelvis through the centre of her, while torrents of honeyed desire soaked her. Her body was a tool of a job she'd never wanted, and over the years she had learned to regard it with dispassionate acceptance, as if it were something impersonal. But now this man was bringing it to life. Transforming it from an aesthetically successful arrangement of bones, muscles, limbs into a finely tuned network of tingling nerves, heat, pounding blood. By making it his, he was giving it back to her.

His fingers circled her navel, making the taut skin of her midriff quiver as shock waves of screaming anticipation zigzagged downwards, and then in a gesture that was more intimate than anything that had happened before he gently laid his flattened hand against her stomach.

For a few heartbeats they were both very still. Lily wondered distantly if he could feel her stomach contract and tighten with clenching desire beneath his palm. Warmth radiated into her from his touch, and she was aware that beneath the storm of need and arousal she also felt strangely still, as if the clamour that had raged inside her for so long was finally hushed.

She felt cherished.

And then the moment was gone, and another crashing wave of need hit her as he slid one finger beneath the silken top of her pants, slipping them down over her hips. She could feel her pelvis tilting upwards in brazen invitation, her head tipping backwards so that he was supporting it in his cupped hand, as the fingers of his other hand splayed downwards, towards the swollen heart of her desire. She felt herself opening for him as his clever, unhurried fingers stroked and caressed, moving inexorably closer, until she could bear the waiting no longer, twisting and writhing her hips in a wordless plea for release.

With a whisper-light touch of a fingertip he brushed the tight bud of her longing, holding her tightly as a shuddering gasp tore through her in response.

'Please, Tristan...' she begged. 'I can't wait any more...'

Her hands were on his shoulders, gripping him tightly as if to anchor herself. She felt as if she were breaking up, slipping away, as if she needed him to hold her and keep her together. Almost imperceptibly he shook his head.

'We can't.'

His voice was hard, jagged, and as he spoke his grip on her tightened as if he had anticipated the rip tide of shock and disappointment that tore through her at his words.

Her head whipped up and she gave a sharp, indrawn hiss. '*Why?* Why not?'

'Contraception. I have nothing.'

The tension left her in a rush. 'But th-that's OK, it's fine,' she stammered, inarticulate with relief, leaning in towards him again and murmuring into his neck as she trailed a line of kisses along the line of his jaw. 'I'm on the pill...and I'm clean... It's quite safe.'

He gave a harsh laugh. 'But you don't know about me.'

His words stopped her in her tracks and she pulled away to look into his face. In the half-light his deep-set eyes were shadowed, making it impossible to read the expression in them. Her gaze travelled slowly over his face. The moonlight turned his skin to marble, and accentuated the sculpted perfection of his cheekbones, the deep cleft in his chin.

She shook her head, momentarily struck dumb by his beauty, trying to find the words.

'No,' she said eventually, reaching out and stroking her hand down his face in a mixture of tenderness and reverence. 'But I trust you. I'll do what you say. If we have to stop this here...'

Her hand was on his chest now. Lily was aware of the steady, strong beat of his heart beneath her palm.

'No.' He barely moved his lips as he said the word. 'There's no need to stop. It's safe.'

Exhilaration leapt inside her, instantly detonating tiny explosions of desire along the winding pathways of her central nervous system. A low gasp of relief and longing was torn from her lips in the moment before Tristan took possession of them, and then her head was filled with nothing but the musky scent of his skin, the champagne taste of his mouth. His hands gripped her pelvis, pulling her onto him, while her fingers tore at his muscular shoulders.

He entered her with a powerful thrust that made her want to scream out with joy. She was taut and trembling with ecstasy, so stupefied with desire that she was unable to think, only to feel. Bliss flooded every cell of her body, making her pliant and helpless, but Tristan's arms were tight around her. Gently he laid her down in the cool sheets, kissing her breast, her throat, finally coming back to her parted, panting lips as the rhythm of their bodies gathered pace and her legs twined helplessly around his hips.

Lily's final, triumphant cry of release shattered the still blue evening at exactly the same time as the finale of fireworks exploded beyond the lake. They lay together, their breathing fast and laboured as the sweat dried on their bodies and pink and gold stars cartwheeled through the blue infinity above.

It had rained in the night.

Getting up from the crumpled bed Lily had gone to the window and looked out onto a cool world of silver and green. The rain had fallen in sheets, turning the glassy surface of the lake misty.

As she looked out of the window of the Jeep as it rattled over the arid African plane just a little over twenty-four hours later it was almost impossible to believe that she hadn't dreamed it. Hadn't dreamed that cool lushness; hadn't dreamed turning away, crossing the floor back to the bed where Tristan lay, his arm thrown across the place where she'd been lying.

Hadn't dreamt the expression of torment on his face.

And as she'd watched him he'd cried out, a harsh, bitter shout of anger, or of pain, and without thinking Lily had slipped back beneath the sheets beside him, cradling his beautiful head against her, stroking him, murmuring soothing, meaningless, instinctive sounds into his hair until the room had reassembled itself in the grey light of dawn and she had felt the tension leave his body.

Then she had got quietly out of bed and put on her silk dress and slipped silently out the door and down the stairs. He hadn't reminded her about the Heathrow terminal, as he'd so jokingly promised. He hadn't woken up to say goodbye.

The Jeep stopped at the camp. The heat was already almost beyond endurance, the air thick with the dust thrown up by their convoy of vehicles. Getting stiffly out, Lily wondered whether she was strong enough to face what lay ahead.

She bent her head, closing her eyes for a second and running her tongue over dry lips.

But she had found the strength to walk away from the tower yesterday morning.

If she could do that, she could do anything.

CHAPTER FOUR

London, six weeks later.

'CONGRATULATIONS, Miss Alexander.'

Lily looked uncomprehendingly into the smiling face of the doctor. She had come here expecting an explanation for why she had felt so awful since picking up a stomach bug on her trip to Africa just over a month ago, but Dr Lee looked as if he was about to tell her she'd won the lottery, not contracted some nasty tropical disease.

She frowned. 'You have the test results back?'

'I have indeed. I can now confirm that you don't have malaria, yellow fever, hepatitis...' he let each sheet of flimsy yellow lab paper drift down onto the desk between them as he went through the sheaf of test results '...typhoid, rabies or diptheria.'

Lily's heart sank.

It wasn't that she wanted a nasty tropical disease, but at least if she knew what was causing the constant, bone-deep fatigue, the metallic tang in her mouth that made everything taste like iron filings, then maybe she could do something about it. Take something to make it go away, so she could start sleeping at night instead of lying awake, hot and breathless, fighting the drag of nausea in the back of her throat and trying to think of that other night. Of Tristan Romero.

She shook her head, trying to concentrate. That was another

thing that was almost impossible these days, but with huge effort she dragged her mind back from its now-familiar refuge in a twilit tower, a moon-bleached bed…

She had to put that behind her. Forget.

'I'm sorry, I don't understand. If all the tests have come back negative, then what—?'

'Ah, not quite *all* the tests show a negative result. There was one that has come back with a resounding positive.' Dr Lee folded his hands together on the desk and beamed at her. 'You're pregnant, Miss Alexander. Congratulations.'

The walls seemed to rush towards her, blocking out the bright September sunshine outside, compacting the air in Dr Lee's very elegant consulting room so that it was too thick to breathe. Lily felt the blood fall away from her head, leaving a roaring, echoing emptiness, which was filled a few seconds later by the distant sound of Dr Lee's voice. She was aware of his hand on the back of her head.

'That's it…just keep your head down like that, there's a good girl. This sort of reaction isn't uncommon…Your hormones… Nothing to worry about. Just give it a moment and you'll soon feel right as rain…'

Rain.

The memory of the lake at Stowell in the misty pre-dawn light rose up from the darkness inside her head; the rain falling in shining, silvery sheets on a landscape of pearly greyness. She remembered the musical sound of it, a timeless, soothing lullaby as she had held Tristan, stroking the tension from his sleeping body, while all the time, unknown, unseen, this… secret miracle had been unfurling within her own flesh.

'There. Better now?'

She sat up, inhaling deeply, and nodded. 'Yes. Sorry. The shock…'

Dr Lee's face was compassionate, concerned. 'It wasn't planned?'

'N-no,' she stammered. 'I don't understand. I'm on the pill.'

'Ah. Well, the contraceptive pill is pretty good, but nothing gives a one-hundred-per-cent guarantee, I'm afraid. The sickness bug you picked up in Africa could have impaired the pill's effectiveness, if that was quite soon after...' He cleared his throat and left the sentence tactfully unfinished.

Mutely Lily nodded.

'In that case it would tell me that it's still very early days,' he said gently. 'There are many options open to you, you know.'

Lily got clumsily to her feet and held onto the back of the chair for support as the meaning of his words penetrated her numb brain.

Options.

'Think about it,' Dr Lee said with professional neutrality. 'Talk it over with your partner, and let me know what you decide.'

She shook her head. 'I don't have a partner. He's not... He wouldn't...' She stopped, her mouth open as she tried to articulate the degree of Tristan Romero's absence from her life without making herself sound like a cheap tart. *I barely know him... I don't have his number and he made it perfectly clear that he wouldn't want to hear from me again... It was meant to be sex without strings. A one-night stand.*

Oh, God, maybe she was a cheap tart. She remembered the hunger with which she'd pushed him back on the moonlit bed and taken him in her mouth; remembered the despair that had sliced through her like forked lightning when he'd said they shouldn't go any further, that he had no contraception, and the desperation with which she had assured him it was safe.

'This is nothing to do with him.' Her knuckles were white as she gripped the back of the chair. 'It's not his fault, or his responsibility.'

Dr Lee's eyebrows rose. 'Miss Alexander—'

'It's *mine*. My fault, my responsibility. My baby.' The words sounded strange and unfamiliar, but as she spoke them the same peculiar, illogical sense of peace that she had felt that night in the tower, in Tristan's arms, came back to her, shivering through her whole body like a delicate meteor shower. She lifted her chin, meeting the concerned gaze of the doctor with a determined smile. 'It's my baby. And I'm keeping it.'

'A call for you, Señor Romero.'

Tristan looked up irritably from the computer screen. 'Bianca, I told you I did not wish to be disturbed.'

'*Lo siento*, señor, but it is Señor Montague. I thought you would wish to speak to him.'

Tristan gave an abrupt nod as he reached for the phone. '*Sí. Gracias.*' He swung his chair round so that he was looking out over the Placa St Jaume and the sunlit grand façade of the City Hall opposite. The Banco Romero de Castelan was one of the oldest and most well established in Spain, and its main offices were in a grand and prestigious building in the heart of Barcelona. It was beautiful, but oppressive. The sun had moved across the square, so that the high-ceilinged rooms with their echoing marble floors were in deep shadow from lunchtime onwards, although that wasn't the only reason Tristan felt permanently chilled when he was here.

'Tom.'

'At last. You're impossible to get hold of,' Tom grumbled good-naturedly. 'Were you in the middle of ravishing some innocent from the accounts department or something? Your secretary seemed remarkably reluctant to let me speak to you.'

'You pay too much attention to the gossip columns,' said Tristan acidly. 'I'm *working*. Believe it or not, banks don't run themselves. Bianca was under strictest instructions not to let any calls or any visitors through, so I don't know how you persuaded her.'

'It's called charm, old chap. It's what those of us who can't get women into bed merely by glancing at them have to rely on. Which one is Bianca? The dark haired one with the cleavage you could get lost in?'

Tristan grinned reluctantly. 'No. Redhead, looks like Sophia Loren, although since you're soon to be a married man I hardly think it's relevant.' His smile became a little stiffer as he said, 'How is your lovely bride-to-be?'

'Oh, you know; beautiful, sexy…and suddenly totally pre-occupied with flower arrangements and bridesmaid dresses. I tell you, it's a whole new world. In my darker moments I have actually found myself thinking that your commitment to anonymous, emotionless one night stands might not be so insane after all.'

'At last you've seen the light,' Tristan said dryly. 'It's not too late to change your mind, you know.'

Tom laughed. 'Oh, it is. Far too late. I'm at the mercy of forces way beyond my control—namely Scarlet and my mother. My mother's decided that we have to have an engagement party and as best man I'm afraid you have to be there. That's why I was phoning—can you manage the last Saturday in September? Scarlet thinks that a small dinner at Stowell will be the least alarming way for her family to meet mine.'

Tristan glanced at his BlackBerry. Parties in Madrid and Lisbon, a business dinner in Milan and an invitation to spend the weekend at the island retreat of some friends were already filled in.

'What if I said no?'

'Then we'll make it October.' Tom sounded completely unconcerned. Leaning back in his chair, pushing a hand through his hair, Tristan stifled a sigh, recognising that he wasn't going to be able to get out of this one easily, but not willing to examine the reason why he wanted to.

'I'll try,' he said curtly. 'But one of the projects is at a difficult stage at the moment. You know what it's like. I can't promise anything.'

'No. Of course not. You never can.' Across the miles Tristan heard the quiet resignation in Tom's voice. 'You are the undisputed world champion of not promising anything and not committing yourself. But pencil it in and try to be there if nothing more important comes up.'

'I'll get back to you,' Tristan said coldly. Cutting the call, he stood up, staring for a moment at the phone in his hand as Tom's words echoed reproachfully through his head.

Every one of them was true, of course.

He swore, slamming his fist down on the polished wood of the desk from which generations of Romeros had run their banking empire, exploiting their name, consolidating their power and their fortune, regardless of who they destroyed in the process. And he was as cold and ruthless as the rest of them. He never allowed himself to forget that or to believe any different, whatever he did by way of atonement. His blue-tinged blood ran thick with the sin and corruption of his forefathers. Of his father. The only way in which he differed from them was that he was honest about it.

Honest.

Honest enough to admit that he was beyond redemption. Honest enough to know that he was best alone.

He gave a short, harsh exhalation of laughter. OK, so while he was being so unswervingly truthful he might as well admit to himself the real reason that he was so reluctant to go to Tom's party. Back to Stowell. Because, he thought in self-disgust, *she* would be there.

Lily Alexander.

The girl with the skin that smelled like almonds, and felt like velvet.

The girl who had caught him at a low ebb, and got past his defences in a way that had never happened before.

And wouldn't happen again, he thought, steeling himself. What did it matter if she was there or not? He would treat her in exactly the same way he treated every other woman he had slept with and discarded. With distant courtesy. And then he would walk away.

Lily's throat was tight and her fingers nervously pleated the rose-coloured silk of her dress. 'A small dinner party to celebrate your engagement,' she whispered. 'That's what you said on the phone. Scarlet, just look at all this...'

She looked anxiously around Stowell's grand hall, where a steady stream of people in evening dress were drifting in through the vast doorway and indulging in an orgy of air-kissing. 'It's like a scene from Georgette Heyer.'

Scarlet laughed and tucked her arm through Lily's, drawing her close. 'I know, I know. Ridiculous, isn't it? We were supposed to be keeping it really small, but in the end I just couldn't bear to leave anyone out, so we've ended up inviting virtually everyone we know.'

Lily felt her heart perform an agonising twist-and-plummet motion inside her chest.

'Everyone?' She slicked her tongue over lips that were suddenly dry and stinging. 'Tom's friends too?'

'Oh, yes, he's worse than me. He's invited just about everyone he ever went to school with, and his entire family.' Scarlet dropped her voice. 'My poor parents are completely out of their depth. You will look after them, won't you, Lily?'

Lily nodded, for a moment unable to speak due to the huge lump of cement that seemed to have lodged in her chest. 'Of course,' she managed at last. 'It'll be lovely to see them.'

That much was true. When Lily was growing up Scarlet's parents had provided her with everything from home-cooked meals to help with schoolwork and advice about boyfriends, and numerous other things that her own mother had been utterly ill equipped to give her. As Scarlet gave her arm a squeeze Lily found herself wondering what Mr and Mrs Thomas would make of her current predicament.

'God, I've missed you,' Scarlet was saying. 'You can't imagine how much I've missed you.' In spite of the diamonds that glittered at her throat and her very sophisticated swept-up hairstyle, she suddenly looked very uncertain, and Lily was reminded of when they were teenagers, worrying about whether anyone would ever kiss them. 'Just because I'm getting married, things between us won't change, will they? We'll still be best friends? Still tell each other everything?'

Lily hesitated, swallowing back the guilt that choked her. 'Of course.'

Sliding her arm free of Lily's, Scarlet grabbed a couple of glasses of champagne from the tray of a hovering waitress. She thrust one into Lily's hand and clinked her own against the rim. 'Here's to us…to friendship that nothing can shake.'

A hot tide of nausea instantly erupted inside Lily's stomach as her newly heightened senses picked up the sweet-sharp scent of alcohol and rebelled against it. God, why hadn't she brought a ready supply of ginger biscuits to keep the sickness at bay? She felt the sweat break out on her upper lip as her throat tightened convulsively.

'Lily? Are you all right? What's wrong?'

Mutely Lily shook her head. In front of her Scarlet's face was a blur of concern and regret sliced through her. For the first time since she was ten years old she was keeping something from her best friend and it didn't feel right. But how could she possibly break the news that she was pregnant when she hadn't even told Scarlet about what had happened that night?

So much had happened so quickly, she thought wearily. She hadn't told Scarlet about Tristan simply because she hadn't had a chance. She'd gone straight to Africa the day after the costume ball, and when she'd returned it had been to find Scarlet starry-eyed and utterly preoccupied with her engagement to Tom Montague. He'd proposed, she told Lily dreamily, at the culmination of the firework display at the party.

Somehow Lily hadn't felt it was tactful to mention what she had been doing at that precise moment…

'I didn't think you looked well,' Scarlet was saying now as she put her arm around Lily's shoulders and guided her towards the door. 'In fact, you haven't been yourself since you got back from Africa. I think it's more than just being affected by the stuff you saw there. You need to see a doctor and get some blood tests done or something.'

'I have,' Lily muttered weakly. They had reached the wide stone stairs in the entrance hall and as they slowly began to descend the cool air from the open doors to the courtyard touched her face and dispersed the suffocating feeling of nausea a little. She took a deep breath, realising that she couldn't really put off telling Scarlet any longer, but not quite knowing how to say it. Pausing to lean against the balustrade at the foot of the stairs, she turned her face towards the doorway and felt the chill September breeze lift her hair.

Scarlet shot her a worried look. 'And? What did he say?'

'Nothing. I mean, I'm not ill.' She faltered, unable to meet Scarlet's eye and looking over her shoulder as she began hesitantly, 'The thing is, I'm—'

She stopped, her mouth open. The crimson walls of the great room billowed and swayed and the vaulted ceiling seemed to rush towards her as someone came in through the huge doors from the blue evening outside. For a moment she thought it was her mind playing tricks on her, conjuring up the image of the tall, effortlessly elegant figure, the perfect, impassive face, in the same way that someone lost in the desert might imagine a verdant oasis in the distance. But then he looked up and she was plunged straight into the pools of his eyes.

This was no mirage.

Frowning, Scarlet turned her head in the direction of Lily's gaze. 'Oh, Tristan's here. Tom'll be pleased,' she said vaguely before turning her attention back to Lily. 'So, what did the doctor say it was, then? The old "too much travel, too much work" thing again? Lily?'

'It doesn't matter.' Lily's voice had dried up to a husk of a whisper. Tristan was coming towards them, one hand loosely thrust into the pocket of his trousers. Every beautiful inch of him, every relaxed, graceful movement declared his utter self-assurance and complete ease, while she felt as if her insides were slowly being fed through a paper shredder. She wondered whether she might actually be about to pass out cold. The idea of blissful oblivion was remarkably appealing.

'Congratulations, Scarlet.' Tristan spoke gravely as he bent to kiss each of Scarlet's cheeks. 'Tom is a very lucky man. You look radiant tonight.'

There had been times in the past eight weeks when Lily had managed to convince herself that her mind was exaggerating the power of Tristan Romero de Losada Montalvo's attraction. During the blank hours of those sleepless nights the memory of his cool, moonlit perfection had taken on an almost mythical quality, mingling as she slid into restless, fragmented sleep with the story he had told her about the moon goddess and Endymion, until she could no longer distinguish reality from fantasy, dreams from memories.

But she had exaggerated nothing, and the beauty of his chiselled angel's face shocked her afresh. She flattened herself back against the stone balustrade, both dreading and burning for the moment when he would turn his attention to her, certain that the secret she carried within her body was written all over her face.

'Tristan!'

Tom's triumphant shout echoed from above, and Lily felt a mixture of frustration and relief as the spell of anticipation was broken. A second later Tom was clattering down the stairs towards them, a lopsided grin on his face. 'You're hardly over the threshold and already you're kissing my fiancée. Have you no respect for the sanctity of marriage?'

Tristan raised his hands in an elegant gesture of helplessness. 'Haven't I always said that you can't hold a woman with a piece of paper?'

'Unless she wants to be held,' laughed Scarlet slightly awkwardly as Tom put his arm around her shoulders and pulled her to him. He dropped a kiss on her cheek.

'Sorry to drag her away, but there are about five hundred distant relations of mine up there demanding to meet her, so you have to release her—just for the time being.' He started to move off, pulling Scarlet back up the stairs with him. Keeping her eyes fixed on the stone-flagged floor, Lily felt panic rising like flood water up from the soles of her feet at the prospect of being left alone with Tristan. 'We'll catch up later once the hordes have been satisfied!' Tom called back from halfway up the stairs, then added with an airy wave of his hand, 'Sorry, you two have met, haven't you? At the summer ball?'

Her heart was thudding wildly. He could probably hear it. God, he could probably *see* it. Heat bloomed in her cheeks as she steeled herself to look into his face. The face of the man who was going to be the father of her child.

His expression was cool, distant, polite. And when he spoke the tone of his voice perfectly matched it.

'Have we?'

CHAPTER FIVE

THERE were people who enjoyed deliberately inflicting pain, as Tristan Romero de Losada Montalvo knew only too well.

He was not one of them.

However, when it came to women he was firmly of the belief that it was necessary to be cruel to be kind, and he had absolutely no intention of allowing Lily Alexander to think that there would be any kind of repeat of what had happened on that hot night in the summer. Or giving her any hint of how much the memory of it had troubled him afterwards.

He watched hurt cloud her slanting, silvery eyes and tensed himself against a sudden rush of unfamiliar guilt. He had expected anger, indignation, a slap in the face—all of which he deserved, and had received from many women similarly slighted in the past. Lily Alexander's quiet dignity unsettled him.

'Yes, we have,' she said softly, almost apologetically. 'I was the girl with...with the dove.'

Instantly her words transported him back to the tower in the dusk and he felt as if the air had been forced from his lungs as he recalled the gentle murmur of her voice, the compassion that shone in her eyes. *And the effect it had had on him.*

One-nil to Lily Alexander.

He nodded slowly. 'Of course.' His lips twitched into a faint, reluctant smile. 'Selene. The girl with the dove.'

Her eyes flew to meet his, and, seeing the cautious hope that flared there, he cursed himself. The golden rules of engagement were keep it emotionless, impersonal and keep it as a one-off. He had broken the first one in the tower, and the consequences of that had been difficult enough to deal with. He certainly wasn't going to break either of the others.

He looked away.

'Yes,' she whispered. 'I wonder what happened to it?'

Tristan paused. The next morning when he'd gone up to the dovecote at the top of the tower there had been no sign of the injured dove, which probably meant it had been taken by some predator in the night. But he wasn't entirely heartless.

Not *entirely*.

'It recovered and flew away, I think,' he said before taking a step backwards and half turning towards the stairs. 'Anyway, it's nice to see you again,' he said with blank courtesy, taking a step backwards and half turning towards the stairs, 'but now, if you'll excuse me, I should…'

For the brief moments that Tristan's gaze had held hers and a thousand wordless images had risen up between them, Lily was aware of the blood rushing to her face, her chest tightening and the breath catching in her throat.

It wasn't a good combination with morning sickness. As Tristan turned away she struggled to take air into her starved lungs as a swirling tide of nausea threatened to drag her under. Groping for the stone balustrade, she felt her legs buckle, and before she could grasp at anything for support the world had gone black and she was falling.

He caught her. Of course he caught her. It would have been too much to hope for that she could just faint quietly, in private, without her humiliation being witnessed by the man who had made it perfectly plain he wanted nothing to do with her. Held tightly against the strong wall of his chest, tugged by powerful currents of sickness and dizziness, she wanted to protest, but knew that the slightest movement on her part could tip her over the edge. And the thought of throwing up all over Tristan Romero's impeccable dinner jacket was enough to make her submit quietly.

He carried her easily, as if she really had the kind of petite build that she and Scarlet used to wish for. Cool air caressed her face, filling her lungs and sending oxygen tingling back into her bloodstream, so that she dared to risk opening her eyes again.

They were outside, walking alongside the wall of the castle. Her face was inches from the hard line of Tristan's jaw, so she could clearly see the tautness in its set, the cleft in his chin, his full, finely shaped mouth. She took a deep breath in, and just the scent of his skin was enough to make her feel faint with longing again. Her body went rigid as she fought to escape his iron hold, desperate to put some distance between her treacherous, needy body and his hard, strong one.

'I'm fine now…I'm so sorry…Please, put me down.'

'Wait.'

The word was a low snarl, and instantly Lily let the fight go out of her as humiliation and despair ebbed back. She had imagined this meeting a thousand times, planned how she would be perfectly reasonable, perfectly controlled and in command of her emotions as she told him the facts and reassured him that she expected nothing from him. No demands, no histrionics, no apologies.

And definitely no fainting.

They rounded a corner and found themselves at the side of the castle that faced the gardens, which lay in a sweeping arc before them. There was a scrolled iron bench set in the shelter of the castle wall; Tristan put Lily down on it, and stood back, looming over her.

She couldn't look at him, not trusting herself to keep the truth from showing on her face. Below, the lake was a disc of black, with the tower in its centre looking dark and forbidding. She couldn't look at that either.

'Better now?'

'Yes. I'm sorry.' Suddenly she was glad that she was sitting down. Adrenaline burned through her, making her feel shaky and spacey as the moment when she would have to tell him rushed towards her with the terrifying inevitability of an express train. She bit her lip and said hesitantly, 'In a funny kind of way it's worked out rather well.'

'Meaning?'

His voice was icy. She could feel goosebumps prickling her bare arms. 'I wanted the chance to talk to you...alone.'

His face darkened, hardened, and he sighed and turned away. 'I thought I explained. I thought you understood that the night we shared—'

'I did. I do.' She cut him off, speaking with soft determination, but her heart felt as if it might burst. *Oh, God...this is it.* 'But I thought you had a right to know. I'm pregnant.'

For a moment he didn't move. Then he took a couple of steps forward, away from her, and Lily caught a fleeting glimpse of his hands, balled tightly into fists, before he thrust them into the pockets of his trousers.

It was cold. She was aware of the chilly iron scrollwork of the bench biting into her flesh through the thin silk of her dress, but she was powerless to move.

I'm sorry. The words formed on her lips, so that she could almost taste them, sweet and tempting. But she refused to speak them. She was used to saying what other people wanted to hear and the habit was hard to break, but the truth was she wasn't sorry. She was glad.

Her own parenting, by a mother who was barely out of her teens, barely able to cope, had been haphazard and inadequate, but it had only fuelled Lily's need to nurture. Her dolls had always been carefully dressed in pyjamas, lovingly tucked into their shoebox beds and read to, even when she had not. For as long as she could remember, the need to love and to nurture had been there inside her, beating alongside her heart, echoing through the empty spaces in her life and in her body. She hadn't wanted to listen to it until that moment in Dr Lee's office when he'd told her the news. The news that should have horrified her, but had actually filled her with a profound, primitive joy.

She wanted this baby. More than she'd wanted anything, ever before.

Slowly Tristan turned round. The expression on his face was like a January dawn in Siberia—dark, bleak, and utterly forbidding.

'Congratulations,' he said, very softly. 'To you, and to the father.'

'*What?*' With a gasp of incredulity she leapt to her feet. 'No! You don't understand. I—'

He turned away from her again, looking out over the garden as he cut through her heated protest. 'I have to warn you to think very carefully about what you're just about to say, Lily.'

His voice was quiet, but there was an edge to it that was like sharpened steel against her throat. Lily felt the sweat cool to ice water on the back of her neck, and clenched her teeth against their sudden chattering, dropping back down onto the bench as her knees gave way beneath her.

'You can't intimidate me.'

To her surprise Tristan laughed; a hollow, humourless laugh, tinged with despair. 'You really don't understand at all, do you? I'm not trying to *intimidate* you. I'm trying to *save* you. I'm trying to give you a *chance*. To give you the freedom to make your own choices, because—' He broke off suddenly. Dragging a hand through his hair, he sat down wearily beside her and dropped his face into his hands for a moment. When he lifted it again the dead expression in his eyes turned her insides to ice. 'Because the second that you say this child is mine, all that will be taken away from you.'

Lily clasped her hands together in her lap, twisting and kneading at her own numb fingers as panic made the words tumble from her mouth. 'I don't want anything from you, Tristan. I don't want your money, or any kind of recognition or admission of responsibility. I was on the pill, but I was ill when I was in Africa, so it's my fault, I accept that completely, but I thought you ought to know that the baby is yours.'

'Who else knows?'

'N-no one.' Despite the mildness of the evening she was

shivering violently now. 'I haven't told anyone. Not even Scarlet yet, but I can't hide it for much longer.'

'You're going ahead with it?'

'Yes!' A white-hot spark of anger glowed in the dark void of her mind at the casual brutality of the question. 'Yes, I bloody well am!'

Nothing penetrated his terrible, glacial calm. 'And you intend to name me as the father? On the birth certificate?'

'Of course!' Her chattering teeth were so firmly clamped together that she spoke almost without moving her lips, her voice a low, furious rasp. 'I *won't* have my child growing up without a name. An identity.'

'No?' He leaned back on the bench, lifting his head and inhaling deeply before turning towards her. His eyes were cold and measuring. 'How much would it take to make you reconsider, Lily? I'm only going to say this once, so I advise you to think before answering.'

'You want to *pay me off*?' Lily gasped, torn between laughter and the urge to do something violent. 'You want to *bribe* me to keep you out of your own child's life? My God, Tristan, you cold, cold bastard! Never. No way!'

His eyes narrowed, but they stayed fixed on hers. 'You're quite sure? Even if it was for your own good?'

She shook her head determinedly as strength and assurance ebbed back into her frozen body. She was on firmer ground here. 'I'm not interested in what's good for me now, Tristan. All I care about is my baby. I want it to know who it is, to have a history. An identity. Roots.'

Things that she'd never had.

In one lithe movement he stood up. The gentle evening seemed to darken as his broad shoulders blocked out the cloud-marbled sky. Slipping her feet from their high-heeled shoes, Lily tucked them up on the bench and wrapped her arms around her knees, hugging herself for warmth and subconsciously closing herself around the tiny, tentative life inside her.

Tristan was standing with his back to her, looking out over

the garden to the dark tower. 'Well, then. I hope you're prepared for the alternative.'

'The alternative?' Something about the way he spoke made the hair stand up on the back of Lily's neck. 'What do you mean?'

He turned. 'It's all or nothing, Lily. If you name me as the father, we have to get married.'

'Married?'

The tenuous thread of certainty that had anchored her a moment ago snapped, leaving her with the feeling that she was plummeting through space, and all logic, all familiarity had diminished to a tiny point in the distance.

Married. The word that, when she was growing up, had always filled her with such wistful hope now sounded cold, comfortless, businesslike.

'But why?'

'Illegitimacy isn't an option,' he said flatly. 'You have to understand that. My family bloodline stretches back, unbroken, for six hundred years. It's my duty to respect and preserve that line. I can't...' here he faltered, but only for the briefest second '...I can't knowingly let a child of mine be born and brought up outside of its heritage.'

Stiffly, shakily, Lily got to her feet and walked slowly towards him. Standing in front of him, she looked into his eyes, trying to read the emotion that darkened them. 'And yet a moment ago you wanted to pay me off?' she said quietly. 'You wanted me and this baby out of your life and your family. I don't understand, Tristan. Why would you do that?'

Their eyes met across the chasm that separated them. His gaze was unutterably bleak, achingly cold, but in that moment she forgot to be frightened or angry and wanted only to hold him. She wanted it so much that she almost felt dizzy.

His lips quirked into a bitter, heartbreaking smile. 'You want your child to have a history?' he said in a voice of mesmerising softness. 'In my family you get six centuries of it, and roots so deep they're like anchors of concrete, holding you so tightly that you can't move. That doesn't give you an identity, it makes it almost impossible to have one. That is why I never, ever intended to have children.' He paused, passing his hand briefly over his face in a gesture of eloquent hopelessness. 'I have no choice about the family I was born into, but you can still choose something different for your baby. Cut your losses, Lily. Get out while you still can.'

Lily's heart felt as if it were being seared with a blowtorch. Slowly, deliberately, she shook her head. 'Our baby,' she said quietly. The ground was cold beneath her bare feet and she was shivering, but her voice was strong and steady. '*Our* baby. I believe in family, Tristan. I believe in marriage.'

Tentative butterfly wings of hope were beginning to flutter inside her. He was offering her the thing she'd always longed for. Marriage; a proper family for this baby—not like the inadequate, truncated version she had grown up in. Not quite a fairy tale happy ending, but a version of it. Hadn't she always vowed that she would give her own children the family life she had never had?

'This won't be that kind of marriage,' Tristan said coldly. 'This will be in name only.'

'What do you mean?' she whispered.

He made a brief, dismissive gesture. 'I have a life. A life that I have carved out for myself against all the odds. A life that I won't give up and I won't share. You'll be my wife, but you'll have no right to ask anything about where I go or what I do.'

'That's not a marriage,' she protested fiercely, feeling the emptiness beginning to steal through her again. 'That's not a proper family.'

As she spoke he shrugged off his dinner jacket and now he laid it around her trembling shoulders, tugging the lapels so that her whole body jerked forwards. 'No. But it's the best I can offer,' he said harshly. 'I can't make you happy, Lily. I can't be a proper father to this child. Find someone who can.'

The deliciously scented warmth of his body lingered in the silk lining of his jacket, and she pulled it closer around her. The unexpected thoughtfulness of the gesture he had made breathed life back into the fragile hope inside her. Looking up into Tristan Romero's dark, aristocratic face, Lily saw the pain there, and instantly she was transported back to the tower; to standing at the window as the rain fell on the lake outside and looking at the watery moonlight washing his sleeping body on the bed. She remembered exactly the muscular curve of his back, the small, shadowy indentation of his spine at its base, the ridges of his ribs. She remembered the tracery of long, pale scars that cut across his shoulders and she remembered the suffering etched into his sleeping face and the anguish in his voice as he'd cried out...

She remembered gathering him to her. Stroking him until his heartbeat steadied, until the lines beneath his brows were smoothed away and she had chased away whatever nameless horrors tormented him. For a short while then, against the odds, she had touched him. She had reached him and he had clung to her. Could she reach him again? Not for a moment, but for a lifetime, for the sake of the baby she wanted so much?

That was what fairy tales were about. About quests that were seemingly impossible, where you had to follow your heart and fight for the things you believed in.

And she believed in love. In marriage. In families and fairy tales. She always had. Raising her chin now, she met his bleak gaze steadily.

'No. If that's how it has to be...we get married.'

He flinched, very slightly, his eyelids flickering shut for a split second before the steel shutters descended again and that small glimpse of suffering and humanity was concealed.

'Right. If that's your choice.' His voice was cold, clipped, but contained a note of weary resignation. 'Just for God's sake don't tell anyone yet.'

'But what about Scarlet?' she protested. 'I can't lie, Tristan—'

'No? Then maybe we should drop this whole charade now,' he said silkily.

'She's my best friend.'

His perfect, sculpted lips stretched into a sardonic smile. 'Then I would have thought that you would be able to see that announcing your own shotgun wedding at her engagement party might not be the most tactful thing to do. You can tell people in good time. For the moment you have to behave in a way that means it won't come as a complete surprise when you do.'

'How are we going to do that?' she whispered hoarsely.

'Just follow my lead,' he said coldly, turning on his heel and walking back towards the entrance to the castle. 'You might not be able to lie, but I hope you can act.'

For a moment Lily didn't move, watching him walk away, his head bent and his shoulders held very straight.

No. She couldn't act, as the director of the perfume commercials would certainly testify. But the thing was, in this case she suspected she wouldn't have to.

'What's going on?'

Tom's tone was as light as always but Tristan knew him well enough not to be deceived. Behind Tom's affable, self-deprecating façade was a mind sharp and incisive enough to have earned him a first at Oxford. He wouldn't be easy to fool.

Leaning against the massive stone fireplace, Tristan took a thoughtful sip of his drink and let his gaze wander around the room. 'Nothing. Why?'

The speeches officially announcing the engagement and welcoming Scarlet to Tom's illustrious family were over, and the guests had stirred and reassembled themselves as fresh bottles of champagne were circulated around. Lily was standing over by the window, talking to Scarlet's parents, who were finally beginning to lose a little of the terrified look they had worn all evening. The light from the fading, flame-streaked sky outside put roses in her pale cheeks.

'That's why,' said Tom gently. 'You haven't taken your eyes off her for the last two hours.'

Tristan's hand tightened around his glass. With some effort he tore his gaze from Lily and looked at Tom levelly.

'Come on, Tom. You're engaged, not blind. She's beautiful. Any man could be forgiven for looking.'

'As long as that's all you do.' Tom softened the warning with a smile. 'Lily's sweet. She deserves a nice steady guy who'll buy her flowers and give her breakfast in bed, not a man like you who'll—'

'Buy her diamonds and give her orgasms in bed?' Tristan cut in ruthlessly. 'It doesn't sound so bad to me.'

'Ah, well, that's because you can't see that there's more to life than money and sex.'

'How little faith you have in me.' Tristan took a swig of his drink and grimaced. 'What if I told you I've decided it's time to give up the one night stands and settle down?'

Tom laughed. 'I'd ask if it was just orange juice in that glass, or whether you've diluted it with vodka like you used to do in school. And then I'd probably look out the window to check for flying pigs and ask myself if it was April the first.' Throwing an arm round Tristan, he slapped him affectionately on the back before moving away to rejoin his other guests. 'The day you get married I'll swim naked around the moat,' he added with a grin.

Tristan didn't smile.

'Deal.'

At that moment he wished very fervently that there were vodka in his glass. And no orange juice. He wanted nothing more than to have something to slow the incessant, ruthless progress of his thoughts and bring warmth back to the frozen places inside him.

A baby.

His gaze moved inexorably back to Lily. She was sitting on the window seat now, deep in conversation with Scarlet's mother. Or rather, he noticed, Scarlet's mother was deep in conversation with her. Lily's head was bent slightly as she listened, her face thoughtful. The gentle, sleepy quality he had noticed the first time he met her struck him again as he watched the graceful movement of her hand as she smoothed a strand of hair back from her forehead.

He felt as if something were crushing his chest.

But it wasn't her beauty that caught him by the throat and squeezed. It was her goodness. Tom was right. She needed a decent man, a kind husband who would love her as she deserved to be loved.

Tristan Romero de Losada Montalvo knew with a cold, bleak certainty that he could never be that man.

He was the kind of man who was effortlessly good at everything he did, she knew that. So it came as no surprise to Lily to discover that Tristan's acting ability was excellent.

It wasn't a surprise. But it was still shocking.

She was acutely aware of his presence, as if some internal satellite navigation system were constantly signalling his whereabouts to her, inexorably pulling her towards him and making it impossible not to keep looking at him. Every time she did she found he was looking back, smiling a little, his eyes dark and glittering with obvious desire.

Acting the part.

And, of course, she was acting too. Standing with Scarlet's brother Jamie, as she smiled and talked and put her glass to her lips she was acting that everything was normal. Acting as if she weren't in the grip of raging pregnancy hormones, that she hadn't just agreed to enter into a loveless marriage with a notorious playboy, and—most challenging of all—that she weren't feeling as if her husband-to-be were slowly stripping her naked with his eyes from the other side of the room.

Husband?

The word was too domestic, too tame to be applied to the man who could make her squirm with guilty longing simply by looking at her from twenty feet away in a room full of people. Married life was going to be extremely uncomfortable if this was the effect he had on her.

Oh, God, what was she doing?

Scarlet's brother Jamie was talking about the band he was in at university. Making vague, encouraging noises, Lily tentatively turned her head to where Tristan was leaning against the huge stone fireplace talking to Tom's gorgeous teenage cousin. The cousin had her back to Lily, but Lily could imagine the expression of slavish adoration on her face from the way her head was tilted up, her whole body arched towards Tristan.

At that moment he looked up, his eyes meeting hers as if she had just pulled on some invisible wire stretching between them. The look was of such smouldering sensuality that Lily felt as if he had slammed her against the silk-covered wall and were holding her by the throat.

And then he smiled.

It was like sunrise. A slow warming, a delicious golden promise of the scorching heat to come. Lily was dimly aware of the cousin looking round, following the direction of his gaze, visibly wilting as she saw that it was directed at someone else.

'Get your coat, Ms Alexander, I think you've pulled a billionaire.'

Jamie's low, amused voice brought her back down to earth. She whipped her head round to face him again, trying to hide her flaming cheeks behind the curtain of her hair, but before she could think of a suitable explanation he dropped his voice and said, 'Right, he's coming over. This is the moment when I slip away and leave you to it. Good luck!'

She wanted to reply; she wanted to tell him to stay, but suddenly her mouth was so dry that the words didn't come. As Jamie vanished into the crowd she turned away, feigning interest in a portrait of an insipid man in a powdered wig with a sour lemon expression. Regency men were supposed to be rakish and dashing, she thought vaguely, remembering the Georgette Heyer heroes that she and Scarlet used to sigh over. They had despaired of ever finding men like that in Brighton...

'This would be a good time to leave, I think. Don't you?'

Her whole body jolted as the husky Spanish voice caressed her ear. Standing behind her, he very gently picked up the lock of hair that was falling over her shoulder and smoothed it back, tucking it behind her ear.

Tongues of flame were licking downwards into Lily's pelvis, making it hard to think straight.

'But I'm staying here tonight...'

'That was Plan A, sweetheart,' he murmured softly, putting his hands on her hips and pulling her against him as his mouth brushed her neck, her jaw, her ear lobe. 'I asked for your things to be brought down to my car. I'm taking you home.'

Lily couldn't speak.

But even if she had been able to she wouldn't have had the strength to argue.

CHAPTER SIX

ALMOST as breathtaking as the skill with which he had assumed the act was the speed with which he dropped it.

Sitting beside him in the low passenger seat, her blood still thrumming from his touch, Lily darted a surreptitious glance at Tristan. The moment they had left Stowell he had distanced himself from her completely, and in the light of the dashboard his face was emotionless. The face of a handsome stranger. She shivered.

'Are you cold?' he asked with distant courtesy.

'No. Well, a little.'

He flicked a switch and warm air caressed her. 'I think we should get married as soon as possible,' he said, effortlessly guiding the sleek black sports car around a bend in the road without seeming to slow down.

Lily clung to the edge of her seat. 'So fast...' she murmured anxiously.

'Sorry.' He slowed down sharply. 'I'm not used to having a passenger.'

A gust of laughter escaped her. 'I wasn't referring to your driving. I meant life.' But as the words left her lips she knew that he wasn't used to having passengers in that either. And that was what she had become.

He showed no sign of having heard. 'What are your work commitments for the next few weeks?'

She shrugged. 'Not much. When I got back from Africa and

I wasn't well I told my agent not to take anything else on. And when I…well, since I found out about the baby…' the words gave her a warm little glow, like a tiny candle, deep inside; gentler, sweeter than the blowtorch of feeling he unleashed in her '…I haven't gone for any jobs. I'm still under contract to the couture people, though, and we're shooting another perfume commercial in Rome in two weeks time. And then, after that I'm pretty free, until the beginning of December…'

She bit back a hysterical giggle. It was as if she were making a dentist appointment, not arranging what should have been the most important event of her life.

'Good,' he said shortly. 'Keep it that way. I'll make all the necessary legal arrangements for the marriage and you can fly straight from Rome to Barcelona for the wedding.'

Lily swung her head round to look at him. 'Barcelona?'

One corner of Tristan's mouth lifted into an ironic smile. 'You're going to be a Romero bride. You have to get married in Spain.'

Her stomach clenched and her throat felt suddenly as if it were full of sand. She folded her hands over her stomach in an automatic gesture of comfort.

Romero bride.

'Of course,' she said hoarsely. 'I didn't think. Your family—'

'Leave them to me.' He frowned, as if something had just occurred to him. 'What about your family? Do you want them to be there?'

'God, no.' Lily swept her hand over the frosted window, clearing a space and looking out into the blackness beyond the cocoon of the car. 'My mother's in some ashram in India, balancing her chakras or something.'

Susannah Alexander had been searching for spiritual enlightenment and inner peace for as long as Lily could remember, but the search had shifted to more high-budget locations since being funded by Lily's modelling income.

'And your father?'

Lily gave a soft laugh. 'I wouldn't know where to send the invitation.'

Tristan said nothing, merely flicking a glance towards the rear-view mirror as he pulled out to overtake a line of cars and accelerate away into the darkness beyond. Lily was pressed back into the soft leather upholstery. The speed ought to have been frightening, but not for a second did she doubt that he was in absolute control of the powerful car.

Of everything.

'What's happening at the beginning of December?' he asked eventually.

'I'm going back to Africa.' she said, unable to maintain her frostiness and keep the enthusiasm from her voice as the words spilled out of her. 'It's early days yet, but I've been asked to be an ambassador for a children's medical charity, and at the moment it's just a case of finding out exactly what I can do, and what issues I can best highlight. I'm just hoping they'll continue to use me because I'd love to give up modelling and do it full time. I've only been over there once so far...' she faltered '...just after we—'

'So you said.' There was a dangerously silky note in Tristan's voice as he cut her off. 'It was where you picked up the bug that put us in our current position.' He gave a short, scornful laugh. 'You can't seriously be thinking of going back?'

A small dart of alarm shot through Lily, leaving a trail of bright anger in its wake. 'And you can't seriously be thinking that I won't!' she said tersely. 'If you'd seen what I saw... Orphaned children, sick and malnourished. Babies whose mothers were too ill to feed them, or even to pick them up and cuddle them; ten-year-old boys forced to take on the role of father to their brothers and sisters, desperately trying to keep their families together—'

'Thanks, but you can spare me the humanitarian lecture.'

He sounded almost bored. The spark of anger flowered into a blaze, fuelled by the anxiety and the frustration and uncertainty of the evening. 'And spare *me* the autocratic alpha male routine!' she hissed. 'You were very quick to tell me that you had no intention of having your life disrupted, but I assume that as *a Romero bride* I'm not to enjoy the same freedom? Well, I've gone along with you this far, Tristan, and I've tried to respect your family and your history because that's going to be the heritage of the child that I'm carrying, but just because you have wealth and privilege and titles doesn't mean you have the right to bully or control or intimidate me.'

'I thought you wanted to keep this baby.' Tristan's voice was icy cold, but in the sodium glow of the streetlights Lily could see a muscle flickering in his cheek.

She sat bolt upright, feeling the seat belt pull tight against her. It was holding her back, restraining her, just like Tristan. Angrily she yanked it away from her body.

'I do! I want that more than anything, I—'

'Then I would have thought,' he said with a lethal softness that chilled her to the bone, 'that you'd want to do what was best for it. Your desire to *help* is laudable, but do you really think that the most deprived and disease-ridden parts of Africa are the best place for a pregnant woman? You were ill last time. Who's to say you won't pick up something again?'

Lily sank back against the seat, turning away from him and closing her eyes as horror at her own stupidity hit her, along with another wave of dizzying sickness, as if the baby too were trying to remind her of its presence. Groping blindly for the controls for the window to let in some air, she mistakenly took hold of the door handle. The next moment there was a roaring sound as the door swung open and a wall of cold air hit them like an avalanche.

Tristan's reactions were like lightning. Steadying the wildly swerving vehicle with one hand, he pushed her back against the seat with the weight of his body as, with an ear-splitting screech of tyres, he hauled the steering wheel round to bring the car into the side of the road. The engine cut out, and the sudden silence was filled by the sound of their rapid breathing.

Very slowly Lily turned her head to look at him. His head

was bent, his eyes closed, and his arm still lay across her body, shielding her, protecting her more surely than any seat belt.

'I'm sorry,' she whispered.

For a moment he didn't move. Then she watched as the fingers of the hand that lay on her thigh curled slowly into a tight fist before he straightened up, placing it with terrifying precision on the steering wheel.

When he turned to her the expression on his face made Lily's heart turn over.

'Understand this, Lily. I will never be a good husband or a perfect father, but I am *not* a tyrant. I will *never* bully or control you.' Just for a second his mask of control cracked and Lily caught a glimpse of the terrible bleakness and anguish that lay behind it. She felt her lungs constrict, sucking her breath inwards in a sort of hiccuping gasp, as all her instincts told her to reach out to him. But it was too late. The mask was back, more chillingly perfect than ever. 'I can't offer you love,' he said in a low voice, 'but I'll give you security. I will do everything in my power to protect you and the baby, and keep you safe. Do you understand?'

Shocked into silence, Lily nodded mutely.

Tristan pulled up outside the Primrose Hill address he'd managed to extract from Lily just before she fell asleep. He looked up at the house—a pretty Victorian town house with a late-flowering rose trailing over the stucco frontage—and then across into the sleeping face of the girl beside him. The streetlight above gleamed on the flawless skin, and cast deep shadows beneath the sweep of her thick eyelashes and sharp cheekbones. It was a composition that would have made photographers and magazine editors the world over sigh with bliss.

Gripping the steering wheel tightly, he exhaled a long, slow breath and closed his eyes.

If only she weren't so beautiful.

He probably wouldn't be in this position to start with, he thought acidly. But even if he was, it would make the role he was being forced into a damned sight easier to play. A business arrangement; that was what this had to be. A simple matter of legality—of a name, and money.

Not sex, because, unless it was of the one night stand variety, sex involved emotion.

And emotion was something he didn't do.

Once, on a long distance flight, he had read a newspaper article saying that scientists had proved that if certain neurological pathways weren't opened up in the early years of life they would never be forged at all. Reading with clinical detachment he had recognised himself in every line, and as he closed the paper had smiled thinly to think that the teary accusations of many of his past lovers were actually now backed up by scientific fact.

Having never experienced love as a child, he was simply incapable of it.

The realisation had brought with it a strange kind of relief, and left him free to pursue his emotionless liaisons without guilt. He was careful, considerate, always making it clear that there was no possibility of anything long term...

How naïve that carefulness seemed now.

With a small sigh she stirred, and he watched her forehead crease into a frown in the second before her eyes flickered open.

'We're home?' she asked softly, sitting up and looking out of the window. 'Sorry, I didn't mean to fall asleep. I'm so tired I could sleep on a clothes line most of the time at the moment.' She bent to pick up her bag, then looked up at him hesitantly. 'Would you like to come in for coffee?'

He felt his eyebrows lift and couldn't keep the sardonic smile from his lips. 'Coffee?'

'Yes, coffee.' She held his gaze. 'I'm a hormonally unbalanced pregnant woman. You're quite safe.'

'I think,' he said cruelly, 'that's what you said last time. I'll pass on the coffee, but I need to get a copy of your birth certificate for the marriage licence. Do you have it?'

She nodded, not meeting his eyes.

Tristan took her overnight bag from the boot of the car while she went ahead of him up the short black and white chequered path. Opening the front door, she switched on a table lamp just inside the hallway and slipped off first one high-heeled sandal and then the other. The light from the lamp shone through the thin silk of her dress, clearly showing the outline of her endless legs.

It was a momentary snapshot, but it was of such pure, concentrated sexuality that Tristan felt the breath rush from his lungs as if he'd been punched in the stomach.

Slamming the boot of the car with unnecessary force, he followed her inside.

The interior of the flat surprised him. He had expected something modern, impersonal—a base for two career girls who spent their time either travelling or partying. What he found was a home filled with beautiful things. Interesting things that looked as if they'd been collected over time, with no regard for value or fashion.

Lily had her back to him and was looking through a drawer in a pretty rosewood desk in the corner of the sitting room. Leaning against the doorframe Tristan looked around. The faded velvet sofa was piled high with cushions in turquoise and raspberry-pink silk, and the walls were hung with a mixture of Victorian oils, modern advertising prints and photographs that demanded to be looked at more closely.

He gritted his teeth and turned his head away.

A grey cat slipped through the open front door and slunk between his feet, disappearing in the direction of the kitchen. Another two, smaller versions of the first, followed.

'How many cats do you have?' he asked, breaking the silence.

Lily turned around, a bundle of papers tied with a faded red ribbon in her hand.

'Officially, none. I'm away too much, but there are lots of strays round here and I feed them whenever I can and keep an eye on them.' She untied the ribbon and took a piece of paper from the top of the bundle. 'That little grey one was just a baby herself when she had the kittens. I feel awful—I should have taken her to be spayed.'

She crossed the room and handed him a piece of paper. Tristan took it without looking at it, then, levering himself up from the doorframe, walked back down the hall, saying with cold sarcasm, 'It's a little ironic, given our current situation, that you're worried about your failure to take responsibility for the contraception of the feline population, wouldn't you say?'

She stopped in the doorway, her eyes downcast, running the length of tattered silk ribbon through her long fingers.

'Yes, maybe.'

Her quiet acceptance sent an arrow of guilt and self-loathing shooting straight into his derelict heart, and he tensed against the acute and unfamiliar pain that flashed through him.

'I'm sorry,' he said tersely. 'That was unfair.'

'No, you're right.' She shook her head, and looked up at him. She was smiling, but her eyes shimmered silver with unshed tears and Tristan felt as if someone had taken hold of the arrow in his heart and was trying to wrench it out. And failing.

Taking the ribbon from her, he took her left hand in his, scowling blackly down at it as he tied the faded silk around her ring finger.

'What are you doing?'

'I need to know your ring size.'

For a moment both of them looked down at her hand in his—pale as milk against the dark gold of his skin, her fingers slender and delicate in his powerful grip. 'You don't have to do this, you know,' she said in a low voice.

Tristan raised his head and forced himself to look at her. 'What?'

'Marry me.'

Her eyes were as gentle as smoke from an autumn bonfire. He slid the ribbon from her finger, unable to stop a bitter laugh escaping him. 'Oh, but I do,' he said bleakly, pushing a hand through his hair. 'I do, you see, because although Romero men don't do love, or...or *fatherhood*, there is something we're very, very good at.'

'And what's that?' she whispered.

'Duty.' He said the word as if it were a curse.

Lily nodded, biting her lip. 'Is that what this is?' she asked quietly. 'Duty?'

'Yes,' he said flatly. 'Duty. That's all, and if that's not enough for you it's not too late to change your mind. But don't fool yourself, Lily. Don't think for a moment that you're getting something you're not, or that you can change me into some kind of new man who's in touch with his emotions because—'

'Ah, but I think you already are in touch with your emotions.' Her voice was thoughtful, almost apologetic. She took a step forwards, so that she was close enough for him to smell the almond sweetness of her skin. Shock juddered through him as she laid a hand on his chest, over his heart. 'And I think the emotion you're most in touch with at the moment is fear.'

It was as if someone had taken a needle of pure adrenaline and stabbed it straight into a vein. Tristan felt heat pulse through his body, closely followed by an ice-cold wave of anger. Circling her wrist with his fingers, he jerked her hand off him, bringing it viciously down to her side so that she lost her balance and fell against him. Her head snapped back, so that she was looking up at him, her face flushed and her eyes blazing with defiance.

With desire.

Tristan felt the blood rush to his groin in instant, primitive response. They were both breathing very hard

'Don't ever make the mistake of thinking you understand me, Lily,' he said harshly. 'I can assure you, you don't. There's only one...*emotion*...I'm in touch with.'

It was a singularly crass, Neanderthal thing to say, but she seemed to bring that side out in him, he thought viciously. He'd expected her to shrink away from the deliberate coarseness of his words. But she didn't. With one hand still imprisoned in his iron grip, she raised the other and gently cupped his jaw.

'I don't believe that,' she murmured.

Afterwards he couldn't have said who made the first move, but suddenly their mouths had come together and her fingers were digging into his flesh as she gripped his arm, her breasts thrusting against his chest. They kissed with a savagery that was totally at odds with her gentleness, and which shattered his memories of the dreamy, languid night in the tower.

She was all things. Anything he wanted, everything he needed at just the moment he needed it most—even when he hardly knew it himself. Her mouth was hard and hungry on his now, meeting the brutal insistence of his kiss with a passion and a fury that matched his own.

But it was he who pulled away, thrusting her backwards and pulling himself upright as he reassembled the barriers of his self-control.

'Then you're fooling yourself,' he said viciously, turning away so he didn't have to confront the bewilderment in her eyes or the broken promise of her ripe, reddened lips.

'You're confusing lust with something deep and significant. You're a beautiful, desirable woman—*hostias*, I'll make love to you a hundred times a day if you want me to, and I'll love doing it. But I won't love *you*. You have to understand that.'

She was leaning against the wall of the hallway, the back of her hand pressed against her reddened mouth. Above it her eyes were huge and luminous with emotion.

'But what if I can't live with that?' she whispered.

'Then I respect that. I won't touch you. I'm not a monster.' His tone hardened. 'But I am a man. There's only so much temptation I can stand. You have to be careful, Lily; if you play with fire, you're going to get burned. It's up to you to choose what sort of marriage this is going to be.'

'A loveless marriage, or a loveless, sexless one.' She made

a sound that was halfway between a laugh and a sob. 'That's my choice?'

He sighed heavily. 'Not entirely. You can also choose to leave me out of your life and the life of your child.'

Her face was half in shadow but he caught the glimmer of a single tear as it slid silently down her cheek. Her hand moved instinctively to her midriff and slowly she shook her head.

'No. I want my baby to have a father, but I won't prostitute myself for the privilege,' she said dully.

Tristan shrugged helplessly. 'OK. Your choice.' Turning away, he began to walk back down the path to the car. 'I'll be in touch with travel details for Barcelona as soon as I have them.'

As he drove away he caught a glimpse of her, silhouetted in the light from the hallway, and felt guilt rise like acid in the back of his throat. Bracing his arms against the steering wheel, he swore tersely.

Why was she letting him do this to her?

He had offered her the only way out he could think of and she had stubbornly refused to take it. He had given her a chance to walk away, to live a normal life, and she wouldn't go.

Why?

Pulling up at a red light, he noticed the folded paper on the seat next to him, and opened it up. 'Lily Alexander,' he read. 'Birthplace—Brighton, England. Mother—Susannah Alexander. Father—unknown.'

So that was it, he thought with a despairing gust of laughter. That explained the fervour with which she'd spoken earlier. I won't have my child growing up without a name. An identity, she'd said, as if having no father were the worst thing that could happen.

He dragged a hand across his face as the lights changed to green, and he accelerated away with unnecessary force. Her naiveté would have been almost endearing if it weren't so dangerous.

Everyone was just a victim of their own past, he thought despairingly.

He wondered how long he could go on hiding how much of a victim he was.

CHAPTER SEVEN

LILY walked down the aisle of the beautiful old church as if she were in a dream.

From behind the snowy tulle of her designer veil the world had taken on a soft-focus haze, so that she was barely aware of the anonymous smiling faces that turned towards her as she passed, the artistic posies tied onto the pew ends, the candles flickering in sconces on the pillars. She just had to concentrate on putting one expensive ivory satin-shod foot in front of the other...on suppressing the ever-present morning sickness...on making it down to the man who stood waiting at the altar with his back towards her.

As she gripped her bouquet of white roses and lily of the valley her diamond engagement ring bit into her finger, heavy and still unfamiliar. It had arrived a week ago, by courier, accompanied by a terse note giving details of her journey to Barcelona.

That was it.

No explanation, no additional words to strengthen the gossamer-fine threads that tied her to the remote, handsome stranger she was marrying. Nothing to reassure her that she was doing the right thing.

Oh, God, *was* she doing the right thing?

'Cut!'

There was a palpable release of tension in the 'congregation' as the director of the perfume commercial stepped in front of her, making slashing motions with his arms. 'Lily, darling, you're walking towards your bridegroom, the love of your life, not your executioner! Some sense of joyous serenity, darling, please! This is supposed to be your wedding! The happiest day of a girl's life!'

'Sorry, sorry…' Lily muttered, gripping her bouquet of slightly wilting roses in anguish. The director's face softened as he peered through her veil and said quietly, 'Look, are you OK under there? Perhaps you'd like to take a quick break? Grab something to eat?'

Lily shook her head. The wedding dress supplied by the couture arm of the company was already so tight it felt like some barbaric method of medieval torture, and a car was due to collect her in just a few hours to take her to the private airfield where Tristan's jet would be waiting. Her stomach swooped at the thought. 'No, really, I'm fine,' she said determinedly. 'I'm sorry, I'm ready now. Let's do it again.'

The director gave her arm a quick squeeze and nodded at the bridegroom, who was leaning against the altar rail talking on his mobile to his boyfriend in Milan. Gathering up her papery silk skirts, Lily hurried back to the church doorway while the director clapped his hands to bring the congregation of extras back to order, hushing the musical babble of Italian conversation that had risen during the hiatus.

Beneath her veil Lily felt the heat of panic rise to her cheeks and breathed deeply, steadying herself against it as she smoothed a hand over the silk that stretched across her thickening midriff. Her heart twisted with primitive love as she thought of the baby inside her. That was why she was doing it. That was why she was shortly going to be getting on a plane and flying to a strange city to marry a man she didn't know. She was giving her baby a father. A name. That had to be right, didn't it?

'OK, people, let's take that again. And remember, Lily, you're drifting on a cloud of bliss, darling. You're in love and getting married to the man of your dreams! What could be better?'

If he loved me back, thought Lily sadly as she stepped forwards once more into the bright lights.

Tristan didn't even glance at his father's secretary as he stalked through her office and pushed open the tall double doors to Juan Carlos Romero de Losada's inner sanctum. He was holding a piece of paper—a printout of the transactions made by the bank in the last week, which he'd been studying ahead of tomorrow's meeting with the chancellors of some of Europe's major banks—and as he threw it down on his father's desk the secretary appeared at the door looking worried.

'*Señor*, I am sorry—'

From behind the fortress of his enormous desk Juan Carlos held up a regal and perfectly manicured hand, the Romero signet ring glinting heavily on his little finger.

'Please, Luisa, it is not your fault. My son has yet to learn some manners.' Settling his face into a smooth smile, he turned his cold gaze on Tristan as the secretary retreated with obvious relief. 'Perhaps you would like to explain what is so important that you neglect the most basic courtesy to my staff?'

Tristan's face was set into a rigid mask of barely controlled anger. When he spoke it was through gritted teeth, his lips hardly moving.

'You authorised a further loan to the Khazakismiri army. Last week. Another four million euros. Do you know who these people are? They're *terrorists*, guerillas, who are responsible for mass genocide.'

Juan Carlos gave a minute shrug of his elegant shoulders. 'Their generals are also very likely to form a large part of the cabinet of the next Khazakismiri government. This is business, Tristan. We cannot afford to be emotional.'

The word hit Tristan like an unexpected blow, reminding him so suddenly of Lily that he felt the air being knocked from his lungs.

I think you already are in touch with your emotions, she had said. *And I think the emotion you're most in touch with at the moment is fear.*

She was wrong, he thought bitterly as he stared unflinchingly into the brutally handsome face of his father; the face that his own echoed so clearly. He knew fear. Fear was the element in which he had lived for the first eight years of his life, until boarding school had delivered him from it. Fear had coloured every day, so that he knew all its shades of blackness. Fear was being small, powerless, not in control, and he had made sure that he was as far removed from all those things as it was possible to be.

'I'm not talking about *emotion*,' he said icily. 'I'm talking about *ethics*.'

'Tristan, this is Spain's oldest and most venerated bank, not some ramshackle, politically correct charity,' Juan Carlos said silkily, and not for the first time Tristan wondered just how much his father knew about his double life. 'Khazakismir is going through a turbulent time in its history at the moment, but it is an area that is potentially rich in natural gas and oil, and when things are more settled our investment will be richly rewarded. I have a duty to provide the best return for our investors.'

Tristan swore with quiet disgust. 'And you think they would agree with that if they knew exactly what kind of atrocities their money was funding?'

'We don't have to burden them with moral dilemmas or complicated political issues. I think of myself as a father figure to our customers,' Juan Carlos continued complacently. 'I make decisions with their best interests at heart. It's not always an easy role, or a comfortable one, but it is my duty. Just as your duty is to the family.'

Just the word 'father' coming from Juan Carlos's lips made Tristan's hands bunch into fists and adrenaline pulse through him. His eyes were drawn, as they always were whenever he had any cause to penetrate Juan Carlos's private citadel, to the large silver-framed photograph that stood on the desk. To the casual observer it showed the Romero de Losada Montalvo family posing happily together on the steps of El Paraiso, but Tristan always suspected it was placed there, not so much to impress visitors, but to remind Tristan of the real nature and extent of his 'duty'.

'As if I could forget,' said Tristan tonelessly, still looking at the picture.

The casual observer probably wouldn't notice the person, standing shoulder to shoulder with Tristan, who had been cropped out of the picture. They would be far more likely to look at Nico, Juan Carlos's youngest son, standing at the front, and remark on the openness of his expression, the infectious charm of his smile.

They would, of course, never suspect what it had cost his older brother to keep it there.

'*Bueno*. Talking of which...' Juan Carlos leaned back in his chair and looked at Tristan speculatively '...I am pleased to see that there haven't been so many unfortunate photographs of you cavorting with unsuitable women in the press lately. I thought that when you gave up that pointless Oxford degree and came to work for the bank that you were ready to apply yourself to your duty as a Romero, but I have been bitterly disappointed by your conduct over the years. Perhaps at last you are beginning to take your responsibilities more seriously?'

Turning to leave, Tristan gave a short, ironic laugh. 'You could say that.'

'Not before time. You need to settle down, Tristan. I hope you're not forgetting the reception tomorrow, after our meeting tomorrow with the European finance committee. Sofia Carranzo will be there. Such a charming girl.'

'By which you mean wealthy, well-bred and Catholic,' Tristan said scathingly.

Juan Carlos's eyes narrowed. 'I hardly need remind you of your duty to make a good marriage. Provide an heir.'

Tristan paused with his hand on the door. 'No. As a matter of fact you don't,' he said quietly.

'So you'll be there?' Juan Carlos pressed. 'Good. I'll look forward to it.'

'Oh, yes, I'll be there.'

As he passed Luisa on the way out Tristan smiled. In a funny way he was quite looking forward to it too.

The light of the short autumn afternoon was fading as the car wound its way through the traffic into the centre of Barcelona. Giving up on the book she had chosen for the journey—Cervantes' *Don Quixote*—Lily sat back in her seat and stared out into the brightly lit shop fronts and cafés, trying to keep her breathing slow and even.

She had no idea where she was being taken, since the enquiries she had made in basic Spanish to the menacing-looking driver who had hauled her bags into the back of the car had been met by a stone wall of silence. Despite the gloom he wore a pair of dark glasses and from beneath these an angry scar ran down his cheek to the corner of his unsmiling mouth.

Lily shivered. There was something intimidating, hostile, in his unresponsiveness that did nothing to dispel the nervous tension that had dogged her since she'd stepped into the plush interior of Tristan's private jet in Rome. The fact that Tristan hadn't bothered to come and meet her himself added a frisson of anger to the apprehension and terrible, treacherous excitement that churned inside her at the thought of seeing him again.

Pregnancy hormones, she told herself firmly. He'd made it quite clear in London what the terms of their marriage would be and she had taken the only option that left her with a shred of dignity. She couldn't accept the alternative, but as the moment of meeting him drew closer she couldn't think how she was going to live with her choice either...

The huge black car slid through streets that grew increasingly narrow, increasingly empty, and Lily twisted the diamond ring on her finger anxiously as she craned out into the gloom, searching for landmarks to give her a clue as to where they were. No one knew she was here, she thought as fear began to prickle at the back of her neck. Maybe the car wasn't sent by Tristan at all, she thought with a thud of horror. Maybe she was being kidnapped by someone who had somehow learned that she was engaged to the heir to the Romero billions…Maybe Tristan was even now receiving a ransom note, demanding a huge sum for her safe release…

Folding her shaking hands protectively across her softly rounded stomach, Lily bit her lip, trying to stamp out the flare of panic that leapt inside her.

No matter how much the demand, the Marqués de Montesa could afford to pay it, she thought with an attempt at self-mockery. This was the man who went to parties by helicopter and sent five carat diamonds by post. *But he doesn't love me,* whispered an unpleasant, persistent little voice in her head. *That's the flaw in the kidnapper's plan. The baby and I are a problem, an inconvenience, and if I were to disappear…*

The car stopped. Lily jumped, her eyes widening with alarm as she saw that they were in a narrow street squeezed between very high, very old buildings. Beside the car there was an archway, its mouth yawning blackly in the gloom. Her pulse went into overdrive. The taciturn chauffeur got out, his footsteps ringing on the stone flags, echoing off the tall walls around them, keeping time with the hammering of Lily's heart as she sat, bolt upright and trembling, in the back of the car. A moment later he opened the door and stood back.

Lily gave a little gasp of terror as she glimpsed a man standing in the shadows of the archway. Instinct told her to get out of the car, that she might still have a chance to run for it, and she stumbled to her feet just as he stepped forward into the dying grey afternoon. He was tall, lean, powerfully built, but even in the gloom there was no mistaking the sharp angles of his cheekbones, the sensual mouth.

'Tristan!'

The breath seemed to catch in her throat, so that the word came out as a strangled croak, and suddenly she was in his arms, burying her face in the hardness of his chest as relief flooded her. He smelled clean and warm and she breathed in the scent, waiting for the wild crashing of her heart to steady.

It didn't.

From deep in the pit of her stomach she felt bolts of heat shoot along her nerve endings as his hands closed over her shoulders, firm and powerful.

'What an unexpectedly enthusiastic welcome,' he drawled with quiet mockery. 'Do I take it you've reconsidered your decision about the nature of our marriage?'

'No!' she exclaimed, blushing hotly as she stepped away from him, folding her cashmere wrap tightly around her and hugging herself to stop the trembling that racked her body. 'I'm just glad that it's you and not some cold-blooded kidnapper with a gun and a ransom demand.' Suddenly the fear of a moment ago felt suddenly silly and childish. 'I didn't know where we were going, and your driver wasn't very forthcoming.'

'Dimitri's Russian. He doesn't speak any English, or much Spanish.' Tristan turned to him and spoke briefly in rapid, flawless Russian, which brought a flicker of a smile to Dimitri's lugubrious features. 'He'll take care of your bags. We go on foot from here.'

Lily had to almost run to keep up with his long, rapid stride.

'Where are we going?'

'To church.'

'Church? The church where we're getting married?'

'Of course.'

A shiver rippled down her spine, excitement mixed with apprehension as the reality of what they were doing edged a little closer. They were walking along a narrow street, just a passageway between ancient buildings, and Tristan was walking slightly ahead of her, his hands thrust deep into the pockets of his black jacket, his collar turned up, demons at his back.

Just looking at him made Lily's legs feel weak.

Another stone archway blocked out the remains of the light for a moment, and then suddenly they were in an open space

again, a small square hemmed in on all sides by a jumble
of ancient buildings, all crammed together as if supporting
each other. In the centre stood a hexagonal fountain, and trees
stretched their branches up to the pewter sky.

'Oh!' Lily stopped, looking around. Apart from a couple
drinking coffee at one of the tables of the bar of the hotel in
one corner, the square was empty. The only sound was the
gentle trickle of water from the fountain, the soft crooning of
pigeons. It was like stepping through a magic doorway, into
another time.

Her gaze returned to where he stood beside a huge and or-
nately decorated doorway set into a wall of pockmarked stone
and she smiled. 'It's lovely—so perfect and romantic.'

The words were met with a mocking twist of his mouth.
'Romantic?' he repeated sardonically, pushing open a small
door set into the tall, imposing entrance. 'I never really thought
of it that way before.'

'Really? You do surprise me,' said Lily dryly, glancing up
at him from under her lashes as she stepped through the door
he held open for her. For a moment he scowled down at her,
and then he gave her a reluctant smile.

'Don't push your luck, Señorita Alexander,' he murmured.
'And remember what I said. If you play with fire…'

'I haven't forgotten.'

Lily followed him into a cavernous space with a high
domed ceiling. Her eye was immediately drawn past the rows
of wooden pews to the dramatic edifice that rose up behind the
altar, of gilded and polished marble pillars supporting a row of
angels with their magnificent wings unfurled, and life-sized
saints in various attitudes of dramatic supplication. Wrapping
her arms around herself Lily walked slowly forward, looking
around, trying to imagine what it would be like on the day of
their wedding…

Now the building was dimly lit and the pews were empty,
apart from an elderly man sitting in the second row, head bent
over his rosary beads, fingers working silently. At the back of

the church a woman was threading long-stemmed red roses and sprays of gypsophila into an extravagant display of greenery on a tall stand, while a small girl played with the flowers at her feet.

Lily watched, noticing the absorption with which the girl held the flowers, the slight frown on her small face as she walked a couple of slow, solemn steps, and realised she was playing a game. She was pretending to be a bride, holding her bunch of flowers in front of her like a bouquet. Lily smiled, feeling a lump form in the back of her throat as unconsciously her hand moved to her stomach, moving over the almost imperceptible bump of her own child.

The past weeks had been exhausting and often joyless, the constant drag of morning sickness made worse by the fact there was no one to share it with, no one to confide in. But there were moments, like this one, when she was struck by the sheer miracle of what was happening inside her body, when the astonishing privilege of having a baby of her own to love and look after almost made her gasp out loud. And she knew in those moments that she would do anything at all to protect it and to give it a safe and happy life.

'Lily.'

She turned her head, and Tristan saw her soft smile fade slightly as she came to where he was standing with the priest. She had been looking at the child, he realised with a stabbing sensation in his chest. That was what had given her eyes that luminescence. When he spoke his voice was flinty.

'If you're ready, perhaps we could get on with what we came for.'

'What we came for?' She frowned.

Aware of the priest at his side, Tristan gave her a smooth, blank smile, hoping that she was sensible enough to detect the warning it contained. 'Getting married, of course, *querida*.'

'Now?' Her eyes widened in shock and colour seeped into her pale cheeks. Grasping her firmly by the elbow, Tristan muttered a few apologetic words in Spanish to Father Angelico as he drew her to one side before she could say anything else that was likely to make the priest have second thoughts about conducting this highly unconventional wedding. It had taken considerable amounts of string-pulling and a more than generous donation to the church fund to silence Father Angelico's doubts about officiating at the secret marriage between the son of one of Spain's most important families and a socially insignificant English non-Catholic girl. Any sign of further irregularity in the circumstances might force him to reconsider.

'Yes, now,' he said, carefully keeping his tone level. 'Or have you changed your mind?'

Her eyes were the dark grey of the English sky before a storm, but whether clouded by anger or by hurt he couldn't tell. 'No, of course not. I just thought…I mean, I wanted—'

'What? A designer dress and a dozen small bridesmaids?' he mocked.

Lily looked down with a sad, self-deprecating smile. 'You make it sound so outrageous. I knew it was going to be a quiet wedding, but I thought that maybe some members of your family could be there, and Scarlet and Tom…'

Tristan wanted to laugh out loud at the idea of Juan Carlos and Allegra sitting passively by and watching him marry this English nobody, but he managed to restrain himself. Taking hold of her chin between his fingers, he tilted her face up to his and spoke very softly.

'It's a business arrangement, remember? You know that, and I know that, but as far as Father Angelico is concerned we are two people so madly in love that we can't wait to marry, so if you really do want to go ahead with this I suggest you play the part of the enthusiastic bride.' He paused, dropping his voice even further, so that it was little more than a breathy caress. 'But this is how this marriage will be, Lily. No grand romantic gestures, no epic emotions, and if you're not absolutely sure you can accept that, then you walk out of here now.'

She said nothing, but her eyes stayed locked on his, opaque with emotions he couldn't interpret, and the silence that wrapped itself around them as they stood close together in the huge, high space was filled with tension. He was aware of his heart beating hard, measuring the seconds while he waited for her to answer.

And then, very gently, she pulled away from him and took a step back.

And then another.

And another.

Tristan felt his stomach twist and the air momentarily leave his lungs as adrenalin hit his bloodstream. Lily had turned and was walking away from him, back up the aisle towards the door, and for a moment all he could think, focus on, was how beautiful she was with the lamplight glinting on her hair and making it shine like a halo of old gold in the incense-scented dimness of the church.

And then, of course, it hit him. What he was seeing. What she was doing.

Walking away.

CHAPTER EIGHT

PAIN shot through Tristan from somewhere, and dimly he realised it was his jaw—that he was tensing it with the effort of not calling out to stop her. Spinning round he looked furiously up at the imposing altarpiece, waiting for the moment when he would hear the door at the other end of the church swing shut behind her, signifying that it was over and he could resume the normal course of his life. The women and the parties. The aloneness that he so cherished.

Didn't he?

It didn't come.

Stiffly he turned round.

Lily was standing in the shadows at the back of the church talking to the woman with the flowers. As he watched she laid a gentle hand on her arm and gestured to the child. The little girl had stopped playing and was looking shyly up at Lily, her expression almost awe-struck.

The mother smiled, nodded. Then Lily dropped to her knees in front of the little girl, smoothing her hair away from her face and gathering her straggling bunch of flowers into a neat posy, showing her how to hold them. The child's small face glowed with pleasure and pride as Lily straightened up again and took her hand.

And suddenly he understood. She wasn't walking out on him. She was doing this her way, with her own peculiar blend of stubborn, determined *sweetness* that made him feel exasperated and guilty by turns.

He felt the tension leave his body, and realised his hands were shaking slightly. Not with relief, he told himself harshly. Nothing so selfless. It was vindication, that was all. Pride. No woman had ever walked out on him yet, and the feeling was unfamiliar. The child's mother, beaming with suppressed excitement, quickly extracted one of the long-stemmed roses from her arrangement and handed it to Lily. Tristan watched as she accepted it, and briefly embraced the woman before stepping forward with the little girl beside her.

She was going to be a fantastic mother.

The thought stole into his head uninvited, causing a wrenching sensation in the pit of his stomach. She had a natural instinct for love and kindness that would make up for his own emotional sterility. And, he thought, watching her walk down the aisle towards him, an inner strength that meant she stood up to him. She lifted her head and her eyes found his. Soft as cashmere, shining with her quiet determination, they held him, and although he wanted to turn away, he found he couldn't.

The priest cleared his throat, obviously eager to get the service under way, and Tristan moved slowly back towards him, his eyes not leaving Lily's. She was close enough for him to see the darkness in the centre of the silver grey iris now, close enough to smell her milk-and-honey sweetness.

Close enough to touch.

His fingers burned with sudden need, and as the priest began to speak about the sanctity of marriage, his mind filled with a taunting kaleidoscope of images and memories that were wholly inappropriate for church: Lily in the field at Stowell, golden and beautiful with her dress blowing up around her bare brown legs; Lily naked in the tower, her skin silver in the moonlight, and the satin soft feel of it against his lips...

From that, had come this.

'Señor Romero?'

They were all looking at him, he realised suddenly: the elderly priest, the little girl, and Lily. Waiting for him.

'*Lo siento.* Sorry.'

Father Angelico looked at him sternly over the top of his glasses. '*Repetid despues de mi. Yo, Tristan Leandro, te recibo a ti Lily, como esposa y me entrego a ti.*'

Almost reluctantly Tristan took Lily's hand in his. The diamond ring he had sent glittered on her finger, sending out sharp rainbows of light in the gloom, and he could suddenly see it was all wrong for her—too showy, too cold—just like the marriage she was about to submit herself to, he thought despairingly. Did she really know what she was getting into?

Of course she didn't. She didn't even understand the vows. He hesitated, and then said in English, 'I, Tristan Leandro, take you, Lily, to be my wife.'

A small smile touched her strawberry-coloured lips.

Father Angelico continued, utterly matter-of-fact, as if he were reading out a report in the financial pages. Tristan felt his throat constrict around the words he had never intended to say. Never wanted to say. As he spoke them to the girl standing before him his voice was a harsh, sardonic rasp.

'I promise to be faithful to you in prosperous times and adverse times, in healthy times and times of sickness.' He felt his mouth twist into an ironic smile. 'To love and respect you every day of my life.'

Lies, all lies. Standing beneath the imposing marble altarpiece in the sight of God and all his plaster saints as he slid the plain gold band onto Lily's slender finger, Tristan wondered savagely what punishments would be visited on him for this blasphemy.

There was always a punishment. He had learned that from a very early age.

The priest was talking to Lily now, enunciating slowly and precisely, and Tristan kept his eyes fixed on the face of a particularly stern looking angel on a gilded plinth as she began to repeat his words in slow, halting Spanish.

Her voice was soft, but it seemed to carry into the high, draughty spaces of the ancient church as she made her promises of faith and love. Empty promises, he reminded himself derisively, but glancing at the priest, and across at the woman doing the flowers, he could tell that they were listening with rapt attention, all openly affected by the tenderness in Lily's voice. Even the old man with the rosary was watching them, his lined face curiously sad.

Tristan looked away again. Staring blankly at the face of that same damned angel, his face a hard, scowling mask from behind which he was forced to act out this charade for the sake of his family name, his blood and his history.

And then she touched him.

As she spoke the words that would bind them together she raised her hand and pressed it to his cheek.

Instantly he felt heat melt the brittle carapace as his gaze was dragged back to hers. Her eyes were like moonlight, gentle and yet so bright it hurt him to look at them, and their soft luminescence seemed to reach into the darkest places inside his head. As she reached the end of her vows there was a moment's pause while the echo of her breathless, slightly hesitant voice died away in the ancient church. But the spell cast by its tenderness remained.

In that silence Tristan bent his head slowly and brought his mouth down on hers in the lightest of kisses.

It was a gesture, nothing more. Part of the act, to satisfy the romantic notions of their small audience, and yet as his lips brushed hers he felt every nerve and sinew in his body tauten as fire blazed through them. He heard the sharp gasp of indrawn breath, felt her arch towards him, parting her lips to welcome his. The rose she held fell to the floor as she slid both hands around the back of his neck so that she was cradling his head; gentle, generous, loving, and the kiss wasn't a gesture any more.

It was hot and real.

As if from a great distance Tristan heard the sound of

applause. It broke into the dark and private world to which
they had retreated, pulling them back into reality. He felt Lily's
smile against his lips as she gently disentangled herself from his
hold, then she ducked her head and dropped to her knees, gathering up her little flower girl and hugging her. Father Angelico
shook Tristan's hand, and then waited until Lily had finished
hugging the girl's mother before leaning across and kissing her
on both cheeks.

Everyone was damp-eyed and smiling.

Except him, of course. Everyone except him.

Darkness had fallen properly outside, and the light from the
lamps on either side of the church door made puddles of gold
on the wet cobblestones in the square. The crisp, cold evening
was filled with the delicious scent of garlic from the hotel restaurant opposite.

Tristan let go of her hand the moment they were out of the
church, and Lily felt the little flare of hope that had leapt inside
her when he had kissed her fade. Her throat felt thick with the
vows she'd just made, her chest tight with the enormity of what
she had done. For her baby.

That was what she had to hang onto. This was a practical
arrangement for the baby. The blistering heat that had turned
her insides into a churning volcano of molten longing when
Tristan had kissed her had nothing whatsoever to do with it.

He held out to her the rose she had dropped. She took it,
unable to look up at him in case he read the shameful need in
her face. 'So what happens now?'

He tucked his hands deep into the pockets of his jacket and
walked over to the fountain. 'I think that wedding nights tra-
ditionally involve considerable amounts of both champagne
and passion,' he said blandly. 'However, ours was hardly a
traditional wedding.'

Disappointment sliced through her.

'No,' she said, unable to entirely keep the sadness from

her voice as she followed him and sat on the stone rim of the fountain. 'Or a traditional marriage.'

'Second thoughts, Marquesa?

His use of the unfamiliar title made her raise her head in surprise. He was standing in front of her, looking down at her, his eyes gleaming in the lamplight. But it was his mouth that held her attention—his sculpted, sensuous mouth, which she hadn't been able to stop herself from looking at all through their brief wedding service. He had a particular way of moving his lips when he spoke that made it look as if he were caressing the words, or saying something indecently sensual even when his voice was quite cold.

'Yes,' she said fiercely.

His brows swooped downwards in a scowl, and he opened his mouth to make some stinging retort. Swiftly she reached up and put her fingers against his mouth, silencing him.

'Yes,' she repeated in a whisper. 'But not about the wedding. About what kind of marriage this is going to be.'

For a moment his face was blank with bewilderment, but then realisation dawned in his eyes, so that their blackness seemed to deepen and intensify. Slowly, wordlessly, he took her hand and pulled her to her feet.

'You're sure? It's what you want, even though—'

'I know. I thought I couldn't bear to take you into my bed... into my body...and know that you don't love me. I thought I could never do that, but now I know that I can't bear *not* to. I'm sure it's what I want.' She rose up onto her tiptoes and brushed her lips against his ear, breathing in the clean masculine scent of his hair as she mouthed, 'And I want it right now...'

'Well, then...' he said in a voice that made her spine melt with longing as he slipped his hands beneath the cashmere wrap, beneath the little top she wore under it. Lily gasped as they met her bare skin and slowly moved upwards, covering her breasts so that her nipples sprang up against his palms. 'It's just as well there's a decent hotel just over there.'

Taking hold of her hand, he began to walk quickly across the square. 'Have you booked a room?' she asked breathlessly.

'No, but I don't think that'll be a problem.'

'But it's a weekend…'

Tristan stopped, looking at her thoughtfully for a second, his beautiful face grave.

'Lily, you have a lot to learn about being a Romero. It has many, many drawbacks…' he kissed her lingeringly on the mouth '…so you just have to learn to make the most of the advantages. Believe me, they'll find us a room.'

'Great Aunt Agatha simply cannot be seated anywhere near the Duchess of Cranthorpe, any of Tom's university friends, or anyone who's ever played lacrosse for Cheltenham Ladies' College first team. I know it's awkward, but we cannot risk a scene like the one at the Talbot-Hesketh wedding last year…' Lady Montague adjusted her spectacles and peered at the vast roll of paper on the breakfast table, weighted down at one end by the silver coffee pot and by the sugar tongs at the other. 'I think if we put her on a table with…'

The names of Great Aunt Agatha's hapless dinner companions remained a mystery as a burst of electronic noise from Tom's mobile phone interrupted his mother. Apologising, he picked it up and read the text message that had just come through.

'It's from Tristan.' Tom frowned, reading out the message in a tone of deep bewilderment. '"One circuit of the moat, this morning. Naked. Photographic evidence required."'

Neither Scarlet nor Lady Montague looked up from the seating plan. 'What *is* he talking about?' said Scarlet vaguely.

'No idea…' Tom's frown deepened. 'Unless…'

At that moment Scarlet's phone let out a trill that made them all jump. But not as much as the shriek of astonishment that she gave a second later as she read the message that had just come through.

Tristan and I got married last night.
Will be in touch soon to explain all.
In the meantime, please try to be happy.
I am.
Love L x

CHAPTER NINE

'OK. So, explain.'

Leaning against the wall of the hotel room, Lily stifled both a sigh and the urge to hang up the phone. It wasn't that she didn't want to talk to Scarlet, it was just she wasn't sure where to start. How to explain.

'I'm pregnant.'

As she said the words she felt the swirling mist of confusion lift a little and certainty flow back into her. That, after all, was the reason at the heart of all that had happened. A shaft of pure sunlight in the midst of the fog.

'Oh, Lily!' Scarlet's tone was warm, but Lily could hear its edge of anxiety and reproach. 'That's wonderful. I mean, *really* wonderful...but, darling—' She stopped abruptly. 'Is Tristan there?'

'No. He went out a little while ago.' She didn't know where. Or why, or who with. He had offered no explanation and she had asked for none. Those were the terms that he had laid down at the outset and Lily understood that she had to abide by them. No matter how hard.

'Good, then we can talk properly.' Scarlet's voice became suddenly businesslike, which Lily felt was a bad sign. 'Look, I'm totally thrilled for you about the baby. Surprised,' she said slightly tartly, 'but I know how much having a family means to you. And that's exactly what's worrying me...'

She let the sentence trail off. In the little silence that followed Lily pushed back the muslin drapes at the windows and looked down at the square below. Directly opposite she could see the high doorway in the scarred stone wall through which Tristan had led her yesterday, the doorway through which she had emerged such a short time later as his wife.

'You didn't have to marry him, you know, honey.'

'I did, actually,' Lily said quietly. 'Don't you see? I of all people couldn't bring a baby up without a father or a name—I know how unfair that would be to the child.' She paused, watching a pair of pigeons bathing in the fountain in the centre of the square, scattering rainbows of shining droplets onto the worn cobbles. 'And it would have been unfair to Tristan too, because of who he is. What he is.'

'*Who he is?* He's a playboy, Lily! *What he is* is a sexy, gorgeous, charismatic Alpha male. *What he isn't* is husband material!'

'He's doing all right so far.'

The words came out without her thinking, but Lily found herself smiling as she looked out into the rain-grey square. It was empty now, silent except for the musical trickle of the fountain, but earlier she and Tristan had been woken by the sound of children's voices—their shouts and laughter—echoing off the high walls. There was a school attached to the church, Tristan had told her, his fingers sleepily tracing a circle of shivering pleasure across the gentle curve of her stomach. The children used the square as their playground. To Lily it felt like a blessing. A sign.

Scarlet gave an impatient snort. 'I'm sure,' she said huffily. 'But there's more to marriage than sex, you know.'

Lily looked at the empty bed that had been the scene of such prolonged, such passionate lovemaking last night, and felt the smile fade and an ache run through her tired, sated body.

Not to this one there wasn't, she thought sadly. Not as far as her husband was concerned, anyway.

Tristan came back in the early afternoon, bringing a blast of crisp autumn air into the warm room as well as several expensive-looking carrier bags. Dropping them by the door, he sauntered over to the bed, slipping off his jacket as he did so and throwing it onto a chair.

Dozing in bed with *Don Quixote*, Lily felt her stomach instantly melt with desire. It was as if in the short amount of time he'd been out she'd already forgotten how incredibly handsome he was.

Incredibly handsome, and incredibly...powerful. His presence filled the room, changing the atmosphere from one of peaceful languor to that peculiar kind of sinister stillness that preceded a thunderstorm.

'What are you reading?'

'*Don Quixote,*' she muttered, feigning sudden interest in page thirty seven, which she'd already attempted to read about four times that morning. Anything to avoid having to confront his raw, menacing beauty.

He gave a short, scornful laugh. 'How appropriate. The ultimate romantic idealist.'

Lily put the book down, bending her head so that he wouldn't see the hurt on her face. 'You've been gone ages,' she said lightly, simply trying to make conversation, but as soon as she'd said the words she regretted them. He turned, pacing moodily back towards the bags he had left by the door.

'It was business,' he said tersely. 'I had a meeting that I couldn't miss.' The words were innocuous enough but tension screamed from every line of his lean body as he scooped up the bags and tossed them onto the bed beside her. 'I stopped on the way home to pick these up for you.'

Hesitantly Lily reached out and pulled the first bag towards her. It was made of the sort of stiff, shiny card that would make Scarlet swoon with delight and as she glanced tentatively inside all she could see was tissue paper. It crackled like the static she could feel in the air as she pulled out the delicate parcel.

'What is it?'

He came towards her, undoing the top two buttons of his shirt with sharp, stabbing movements. Lily felt her breath stall.

'Have a look.'

She wanted to, but that meant tearing her eyes away from the strip of olive skin that was being revealed at his throat. Blindly her fingers fumbled with the paper, until they met cool, slippery satin. She looked down.

The dress was the colour of old ivory, or bone. For a moment she just gazed down at it lying against her bare legs, looking almost incongruously expensive and precious in the rumpled chaos of the bed.

'Tristan, it's beautiful...but why?'

A guilt present? Had the meeting that was so important been with one of his women...his mistresses? That would explain the dangerous tension that lay just beneath the surface, and the glitter in his eyes.

'Because you didn't get your white dress yesterday.'

Lily felt her eyes sting with the threat of sudden tears. He had done it again. Every time she just about convinced herself that she could live by his cold rules and keep her own treacherous feelings hidden he brought her resolve crashing down by doing something unexpectedly, unfairly lovely. Slowly unfolding her cramped legs, she got unsteadily to her feet, so that she was standing on the bed in her tiny vest top and knickers and holding the dress up against her. It was simple and exquisite—short and close-fitting with a low neckline that swept almost from shoulder to shoulder. She let it fall again and walked across the tangle of covers towards him and bent down to wrap her arms around his neck.

'Thank you. You didn't have to do that.'

Raised up by the height of the bed, her stomach was almost level with his face and for a second she felt him rest his head against it. Then he stiffened, pulling away and turning his back on her.

'Actually I did. You'll need something to wear tonight, and I wasn't sure you would have brought anything smart enough.'

'Smart enough for what?'

He turned back to face her, and the expression on his face

made her heart stop. She wasn't sure whether it made her want to run away from him, or to take him in her arms as she had done that night in the tower.

'A black tie reception for a few European chancellors and bankers at El Paraiso.'

'El Paraiso?' she echoed, her heart sinking.

'My parents' house.'

There was something oddly flat in the way he said the words, as if he was being very careful not to let any feeling seep into them. Lily remembered him standing in the garden at Stowell the evening she'd told him about the pregnancy. *I have no choice about the family I was born into*, he'd said, and his voice had vibrated with all the emotion he was being so careful to keep in check now.

'Ah,' she said softly, stepping down from the bed and walking towards him with a demure smile. 'A black-tie reception for Europe's major financiers, and meeting your parents. Sounds like a fun evening. I can see now why the "gorgeous-dress-as-bribe" was necessary, because otherwise I might just decide I need to catch up on some of the sleep we missed out on last night and spend the evening in bed.'

She came to a standstill in front of him, looking up at him without really lifting her head. He seemed so tall, so very lean and strong and well muscled, but somehow that just seemed to emphasise the hollowness in his eyes. There was a bitter edge to his smile.

'Not a chance. Technically you're my wife now, remember?'

'Of course.' She placed her hands flat against his chest, feeling the steady beat of his heart. Her whole body ached with the longing to put her arms round him and soothe away the tension, but she already understood him well enough to know that he was too proud to lower his guard for such an obvious approach.

Wide-eyed, she looked up at him. 'And as your wife,' she said very gravely, 'I suppose it's my *duty* to accompany you?'

'Exactly.' His smile widened a little. 'You're catching on fast.'

'OK, then, let's compromise.'

His eyebrows rose. 'Meaning?'

Lily rolled her eyes in an exaggerated display of exasperation. 'Compromise?' she said emphatically as if she were talking to a small child, while all the time slowly undoing the buttons of his shirt. 'It means each of us getting a little bit of what we want. I believe it's widely held to be one of the essential ingredients in a marriage—although I'm not sure if the same principles apply to marriages of convenience. However, I think, just to be on the safe side, that we'd better assume that they do.'

'So, let me guess—you want to spend a little bit of the evening in bed?'

'Now look who's catching on fast,' Lily said huskily, grasping hold of the edges of his open shirt. 'A little bit of the evening, and most of the afternoon too...'

He was smiling broadly as he lifted her up and laid her on the bed, and the anger and the pain that shadowed his eyes had dissolved away leaving clear, gleaming pools of pure desire. Lily's tender heart blossomed and ached as she lay back against the pillows. Leaning over her, Tristan impatiently tore off his shirt while he trailed a path of kisses over her collarbone and down her arm.

The light of the pale autumn sun slanted through the window, brushing Tristan's smooth butterscotch skin with gold dust, and highlighting the faint cross-hatching of scars on his back.

Lily bit her lip, closing her eyes and sliding her hand into his hair, her whole body throbbing with love and need while simultaneously being racked with pain.

Pain that she sensed in him and longed to heal, if only he'd let her near.

But he wouldn't. She gasped as he took her hips between his big hands and brought his mouth down on her navel, kissing, sucking, moving his mouth lower...

This was the only closeness she was allowed, and while

she craved it with every cell of her being she also knew that it wasn't enough. It would *never* be enough.

She wanted what she could never have.

Not just his body, but his heart.

Modelling would never have been Lily's first choice of career. She had fallen into it thanks to a combination of chance and financial necessity, shelving her dreams to go to university in order to make the most of the undreamt of riches that were suddenly within her reach.

But at times like this, she reflected hazily as she walked with Tristan across the grand entrance hall at El Paraiso, she was glad that she had. Confidence was easier to fake if you knew how to hold yourself and how to walk.

Although, given the thoroughness with which Tristan had just made love to her, that wasn't exactly easy. Especially not in four inch heels, and with Tristan, mouthwateringly handsome in black tie, so close beside her. Close enough that she could smell the clean scent of his skin from the hasty, last minute shower they had shared while Dimitri had waited for them in the car below. Close enough to sense the tension in his body, despite his outward show of utter indifference.

They were late.

Lily's heels made a rapid, staccato rhythm on the marble floor as she struggled to keep up with him. Silently she cursed the fact that she'd spent the car journey here staring into the blackness of the window while her mind mentally replayed the blissfully erotic events of the afternoon in glorious freeze-frame detail, rather than asking Tristan to fill her in on his family. Too late now, she thought in panic. From behind double doors between the symmetrical sweeping staircases that rose on either side of the hallway, she could hear the sound of voices, and her chest constricted with nerves.

'Wait,' she croaked, putting an arm on his sleeve.

Tristan stopped. He was composed to the point of complete detachment, far removed from the man who had buried his face in her neck and gasped her name just an hour earlier. 'Are you OK? You don't feel sick?'

Lily gave a half-laugh and pressed her hand to her stomach. 'Yes, but then I do all the time. It's not that, it's just...' she twisted nervously at a strand of hair that had escaped the pins that held it in a sophisticated twist on top of her head '...I'm about to meet your family and I don't know anything about them.'

'Believe me, that's a good thing,' he said acidly, his face hardening as he looked in the direction of the doors in front of them.

'Tristan, don't,' Lily said in anguish. 'I mean—for example, do you have any brothers and sisters?'

He flinched. Only slightly, but she caught the minute narrowing of his eyes, the tiny indrawn breath. 'Yes. I have...one brother. Nico. He's in Madrid, so he won't be here tonight. Now, if that answers your questions, perhaps we could go in?'

He moved to open the door, but Lily stayed where she was, fighting the nerves that were shredding her insides.

'Tristan?'

'What?' He spun round, not bothering to conceal his impatience. She was standing in the middle of the oppressively grand hallway, her chin lowered, her hands plucking nervously at her dress.

The dress he'd chosen for her earlier, sensing without knowing much about such things that the colour would bring out the pale gold of her skin, and that the low scooped neck would show off the fragile perfection of her collarbones.

It did.

Dios mio, it did...

She bit her lip, looking up at him with smoky, hesitant and unreasonably lovely eyes. 'Do I look OK?'

Tristan stiffened, straightening his shoulders, his head jerking back slightly as he forced back the almost overwhelming urge to cross the stretch of marble floor between them and take her in his arms and kiss her until her lips were bare of gloss and her hair had tumbled from its pins.

He pushed open the door. 'You look fine,' he said tonelessly. 'Now, let's get this over and done with.'

Lily had never seen a room so luxurious or so chilling.

Long, high-ceilinged and decorated entirely in shades of cream and gold, it made Stowell, with its faded silks and threadbare Persian rugs, look positively down at heel by comparison. And although Scarlet frequently joked about the drafts there, Lily felt an icy chill creep down her spine as she followed Tristan into the crowded room. It was as if the temperature had just dropped several degrees, and almost without thinking Lily felt for Tristan's hand as they made their way through the crowd towards a group of people at the far end of the room.

She couldn't be sure exactly how she knew that the tall man with his back to them was Tristan's father. Perhaps it was something to do with the breadth of his shoulders, a certain arrogance in the tilt of his head that was already familiar. He was talking to another man, gesturing eloquently, confidently with a hand that held a crystal champagne flute. Beside them two women—one about Lily's age in an impeccable but rather conservative little black dress, one older and wearing a high necked dress in midnight blue—stood mutely.

Draining her glass, the older woman looked up suddenly. She was slender, elegant and immaculately made up in a way that obscured rather than enhanced her considerable beauty. As she saw them a look—shock? fear?—flickered across her face. Before Lily had time to put her finger on what it was, it was gone; replaced by a gracious smile of welcome.

'Tristan, darling boy! You're here!'

Juan Carlos Romero de Losada turned round slowly, flicking back the cuff of his expensively tailored jacket and checking his watch before looking at his son.

'At last,' he said with a sinister smile. 'You are precisely one hour and five minutes late.'

Tristan ignored him, leaning across to kiss both women, but Lily felt his hold on her hand tighten. 'Good evening, Mama, Sofia...' His lips twitched into the ghost of a smile. 'Sorry we're late. We rather lost track of time.'

Lily was aware of all eyes turning in her direction. Her heart was crashing against her ribs as Tristan raised her hand so that everyone could see her fingers laced through his, with the diamond glittering beside her new wedding band. Slowly he brought it to his lips, kissing it gently before saying, 'I'd like to introduce Lily Alexander. My wife, and the new Marquesa de Montesa.'

For a second it seemed that a spell had fallen on the small group. While all around them the rest of the guests talked and laughed and drank the excellent vintage cava, no one in the circle around the fireplace moved or spoke. Lily glanced at Juan Carlos and felt a sickening thud of horror as she saw the fury rising in his eyes like some dark liquid coming to the boil. Fury that in this setting, in front of his guests, he was powerless to express.

It was Tristan's mother who broke the terrible silence, stepping forward and kissing Lily on both cheeks with a blast of designer perfume and alcohol fumes.

'But, my dear, how delightful! You must forgive us for being so unmannerly, but this is such a shock. I had almost given up hoping that Tristan would settle down—and with such a beautiful girl.' She gave an awkward little laugh. 'It is almost too much to take in!'

As Lily submitted to Allegra Montalvo y Romero de Losada's gracious embrace she had the strangest feeling that she were floating amongst the painted clouds and cherubs on the ceiling, looking down on the tableau of figures below. Sofia, whose olive skin had flushed with telltale colour when Tristan had kissed her cheek, now seemed to stiffen and shrink backwards, clearly desperate to move away. Tristan's father, the oddly compelling Juan Carlos, stepped forward to take Lily's hand in his.

For an awkward moment she stood, one hand still clasped in Tristan's, one imprisoned between Juan Carlos's soft fingers. She could almost feel the animosity between the two men crackling through her, as though she were some kind of conductor.

'Lily...Alexander?' Juan Carlos repeated quietly, with a smile that didn't quite reach his eyes. 'I think our paths have not crossed before?'

It was a clever question, Lily thought with a stab of anguish. Everyone must have been thinking the same thing—that the idea of her ever having brushed even the most outward peripheries of Juan Carlos's exclusive social circle was utterly preposterous. Sofia gave a strange snort of amusement, which she quickly suppressed with a swig of cava.

'No,' she said quietly. 'I don't think so.'

'No. Of course,' Juan Carlos continued softly, 'I would have remembered such a pretty face. You must tell us all about yourself—where you come from and what you do for a living.'

'I'm a model. I live in London.'

From the look on Juan Carlos's patrician face it was as if Lily had said she was a high class hooker. His brows rose almost into his distinguished grey-streaked hair.

'My dear, how fascinating. What surprising people my son seems to mix with. And where did you meet?'

'At Tom's,' Tristan said coldly. 'At a party in the summer.'

Allegra's exclamation of delight sounded almost genuine. 'How romantic!' she exclaimed a little too brightly. 'And how sudden. It must have been love at first sight!'

Frowning a little, Tristan tucked the stray lock of hair behind Lily's ear. 'I don't remember it being *love* at first sight. I don't think that came until we woke up the next morning.'

Lily was aware of the brittle tinkle of Allegra's laugh, but only distantly.

A shiver of helpless longing rippled across Lily's skin—skin that still tingled from the ecstasy he had awoken in her earlier. But she was aware that beside her Juan Carlos's face had taken

on a bland and dangerous look. Giving an abrupt nod in the
direction of the ladies, he turned to Tristan.

'A word in private, if you please.'

For a moment Tristan hesitated, as if he was going to argue,
and then Allegra stepped forward and tucked her arm through
Lily's.

'You men go and talk business! I'm going to show Lily
around our home, and get to know her properly.'

'I assume she's pregnant?'

In the masculine enclave of Juan Carlos's wood-panelled
office there was no place for such feminine refinements as
champagne flutes and cava. Picking up a solid, square cut de-
canter from a cedarwood tray, Juan Carlos sloshed dark liquid
into two glasses. He held one out to Tristan, who ignored it.

'And why would you assume that?'

Juan Carlos looked at him over the rim of his glass. 'Because,'
he said with slow, unpleasant relish, 'I can't think why else you
have married her. Women like that are mistresses, not wives.'

*Don't react. Don't show him that he's got to you. Don't let
him see that it hurt.* It was the mantra that had echoed through
Tristan's head countless times before when he'd stood in this
room. No doubt at some point during all those years the ability
to conceal his emotions successfully had gone from being an
effort of will to being a habit.

With deceptive nonchalance he leaned against one corner of
Juan Carlos's impressive desk and raised his eyebrows slightly.
'Women like that?'

'Women with no breeding,' Juan Carlos said dismissively,
taking a mouthful of his drink and giving a grimace that Tristan
understood was not directed at the excellent brandy. 'A *model*,
Tristan! Such a cliché.' He looked down into his glass, swirling
the liquid around for a moment before saying quite conversationally, 'I take it you are doing this to deliberately undermine
me?'

'Just like you undermined me at the meeting this morning?'

Tristan said with quiet contempt. 'How did you get those men to vote with you—against me—on increasing the interest on the African loans? That money is going to come straight out of that country's healthcare budget or education, or farming subsidies, as everyone in that meeting knew. How much did you have to pay them for their votes?'

Juan Carlos moved round to the other side of the desk and sank into the huge leather chair. 'Not everything comes down to money,' he said thoughtfully, examining his manicured fingernails. 'Most things, but not all.'

'Oh, *Dios*… Sofia.' Tristan got up from the desk and took a few paces, thrusting his hand through his hair as his mind raced. 'The deal was to do with me and Sofia, wasn't it?'

'Would that be such a bad idea? Do you think I married your mother for love?'

'No.' Tristan's laugh was edged with bitterness and despair. 'No, I *never* thought that.'

Acid burned at the back of his throat and the darkness that he constantly felt crouched around him encroached a little further. It was something that he was used to—he had lived with it for as long as he could remember, without ever really wanting to look directly at it, or give it a name. Until now. Standing here, in the room that had been the scene of so much suffering, he remembered again Lily's soft voice, the warmth of her hand on his heart. *The emotion you're most in touch with at the moment is fear…*

He hadn't wanted to admit she was right. He hadn't even wanted to consider the possibility.

But suddenly he knew she had been absolutely spot on. Looking into the empty eyes of his father, so similar to the ones that looked back at him from the mirror every morning, he was afraid.

For a long time he had accepted that because of the man in front of him he wasn't able to love. Neurological fact. But for the first time he allowed himself to look right into the blackness and confront what had been lurking there all the time; the fear that where there should have been love, all the cruelty and the coldness of those crucial early years had been hardwired into his brain instead. What if it was there, waiting for an outlet, and when Lily had this child…?

Dios, oh, Dios, what had he done?

He had forced her into this out of his innate sense of family honour, but what about her? What about his duty to her and to the baby? He had promised to protect her and keep her safe, but how could he do that if the biggest danger she faced was from him? She made him feel things that scared him. Things that he knew he couldn't control.

He had told her that he wasn't a monster. But what if he was? What if he was just like his father and he didn't know it yet?

His fists were tight balls of tension, and he pressed them to his temples as Juan Carlos's quiet, eminently reasonable voice washed over him.

'It would have been a brilliant match, surely you can see that? A link between our bank and the largest privately owned bank in Greece. Sofia would have been a good wife, and you could have had your sordid little affairs with models on the side.' He paused and shook his head uncomprehendingly. 'But instead you *married* one. It's a shame, Tristan—I thought you were more in control of your emotions. I thought you were too sensible to get carried away by stupid notions of romance.'

'I didn't,' Tristan said icily. 'You were right first time. Our marriage has nothing to do with emotion or romance. Lily is pregnant, and I'm doing my duty—to her and to our ancient, rotten, noble *family*.'

From the other side of the desk he saw something gleam in his father's cold eyes, and thought it might be triumph. 'She trapped you into this deliberately,' said Juan Carlos harshly.

Walking towards the door, Tristan laughed—a sound as hollow and bleak as his own heart. 'I think she's the one who's been trapped, don't you? Trapped into a loveless, sterile, dutiful marriage.'

'Hardly,' said Juan Carlos pompously. 'You are a Romero—the Marqués de—'

Tristan opened the door. 'Exactly,' he said, with bitter resignation. 'Who in their right mind would want anything to do with that?'

'You have a lovely home,' Lily said awkwardly as she stood in the small sitting room in Allegra's private suite of rooms. It seemed that they had come a long way from the large, crowded place where the reception was being held. This room, with its thick, thick carpets, quilted sofas, acres and acres of swagged silk curtain, was in a different world entirely: still opulent, still expensive, but warm and comfortable to the point of being suffocating. Lily was beginning to feel faint.

Allegra smiled and took another mouthful of cava. 'Thank you. I hope that in time you will come to think of it as your home too. None of the children spend much time here any more, but maybe...' She faltered, and Lily glanced sharply up.

'None of them?'

'Sorry.' With a little laugh, Allegra shook her head and waved her glass in a sweeping arc. 'I mean *neither* of them. Maybe now he is married Tristan will have more time. He's always so busy, you see...'

The words faded and she looked around, as if trying to remember why they were there. Lily was wondering the same thing. Allegra Montalvo y Romero de Losada was beautiful, glamorous, generous and welcoming, but she was also extremely drunk. From the fact that this hadn't been immediately apparent at the reception, Lily realised that it was a state of affairs Allegra was obviously quite used to. She also thought that it probably explained the rather large bruise that was discernible on one of her elegant cheekbones, beneath the pancake make-up.

'I think,' said Lily carefully, 'that perhaps I'd better be getting back. Tristan will be wondering where I've got to.'

Would he?

Once again her mind wandered back to the afternoon. There had been a fervour to his lovemaking that was almost fierce in its intensity. A ripple of profound, private delight shimmered through her as she recalled it…

'Wait! You can't go until I've given you what I brought you up here for,' Allegra said, sashaying into the bedroom and disappearing into another small room leading off it. Left alone, Lily pressed her palm over the tiny roundness of her bump and silently pleaded with the baby to ease up on the sickness. The waves of nausea were getting closer together now, each one threatening to tip her right over…

'Here!' Allegra was back, holding a large, flat box out in one hand and her glass in the other. It was full again, Lily noticed with concern. She must have bottles stashed all over the place.

Allegra set the box on the low table and sat back on one of the feather sofas. 'Open it.'

Lily approached the box warily as if it were likely to contain something highly explosive, or liable to scuttle out and sting her. Lifting the tooled leather lid, she felt as if she were in one of those children's cartoons where the characters opened the treasure chest and their faces were illuminated with the glow of the gold, only now the light coming from the treasure wasn't a yellow glow, but a shimmering meteor shower of bright rainbows from the collar of ruby and diamonds that lay against the black velvet.

Allegra was watching her face. 'You're a Romero now,' she said quietly, and suddenly she sounded absolutely sober. 'A Romero bride, just as I was all those years ago. These are the Romero jewels, so it's only right that they should be passed on to you.'

Lily's hand had automatically flown to her mouth when she'd first seen the diamonds, but she dropped it now and tried to speak. 'Oh…*señora*….'

'Please, call me Allegra.'

'Allegra, I can't accept these,' she protested a little breathlessly. 'They're beautiful—more beautiful than anything I've ever seen, but so expensive…'

'Priceless.' Allegra got up, swaying very slightly as she leaned forward and picked up the necklace. 'But you already have my son, Lily, and although he might not think it he is worth so much more to me than these are. Please, let me put them on.'

The stones felt very cold against Lily's bare skin, and Allegra's long fingernails scraped at her neck as she struggled with the clasp. Lily closed her eyes, fighting back the rising nausea and the feeling that she was being strangled…suffocated…

'There.' With a triumphant flourish Allegra stood back and, taking Lily by the hand, led her over to a mirror that hung on the wall.

The collar was wide, seeming to elongate her neck, and the large diamonds glittered with a brilliance that dazzled her. In the centre a single ruby nestled exactly in the hollow at the base of her throat, and it looked like a drop of blood.

Lily jumped slightly as Allegra's face appeared beside hers in the mirror, and with a strange, dreamlike expression Allegra removed Lily's own cheap costume earrings and slipped a pair of ruby droplets in their place.

'I…I don't know what to say…' she said, truthfully. She felt a little faint, a little dizzy and it was taking all her energy just to suppress the sickness. Allegra's fingers bit into her flesh a little too hard as she held Lily in front of the mirror.

'Welcome to the family, Lily,' she said in a strange, choked voice. 'I hope that—'

She didn't get any further. At that moment the door opened, and Tristan appeared.

'There you are.'

He stopped, and although his expression didn't change much there was something about the stillness that suddenly seemed to come over him that made Lily's heart batter against her ribs. In the light of the silk-shaded lamps he looked very pale.

And terrifyingly angry.

Allegra stepped back, away from Lily. 'Tristan, we were just—' she began, falteringly and then started again. 'The Romero jewels belong to Lily now.'

Tristan didn't look at her. Not for a second did his eyes leave Lily. They glittered with a dark brilliance like the diamonds.

'Take them off,' he said in a voice of frosted steel.

'It's so kind of your mother,' Lily said breathlessly, but her throat tightened around the words and she got no further. Her heartbeat drummed in her ears, and an icy mist of horror and panic seemed to be closing around her, blurring everything that was familiar and normal and logical.

'Take. Them. Off,' he snapped. *'Now.'*

Understanding tore into her head like a cyclone. Her fingers flew to the clasp and shakily fumbled with it. Of course, she thought despairingly, of course. He was telling her she had no right to wear the priceless Romero jewels. Her chest burned with the effort of breathing and acid tears gathered behind her eyes as the clasp opened and the necklace slithered off in a shimmer of brilliance that only real diamonds gave off.

Their marriage was a sham. Paste and plastic. Not real. The Romero jewels belonged around the neck of a woman Tristan loved, a woman he had willingly taken to be his bride, not the one who had trapped him into it.

She handed them back to Allegra, opening her mouth to say something, but discovering that she didn't know what to say. Thank you?

Sorry?

In the end she settled instead for a frozen little smile before following Tristan from the room.

'Well, that went well, then.'

It was a pretty feeble attempt at humour, Lily knew that. She couldn't blame Tristan for completely ignoring it and keeping his stony face turned towards the blank, dark window of the car. But still it left the problem of the gaping chasm that had opened up between them. The closeness they had shared this afternoon now seemed about a million years ago. Miserably she tried again.

'Tristan, I'm sorry. I didn't know that she was going to do that, and I wasn't going to—'

'Forget it.' His voice stung her like the lash of a whip. He took a deep breath, regaining his formidable self-control again before saying, 'It's not your fault.'

There was a terrible finality in his voice and he kept his face turned away. His profile looked as if it had been carved in ice.

Not her fault. Of course not. She couldn't help what she was, or, more importantly, what she wasn't—aristocratic, well-connected, with a string of surnames that would never fit in the strip on the back of a credit card, and a Christmas-card list that included all the crowned heads of Europe.

And that was what all this was about.

She had failed to pull it off, this business of being the Romero bride. Her face might have graced some of the most prestigious magazine covers in the world, but it had failed to fit in the Romeros' exclusive circle. Juan Carlos hadn't bothered to pretend, and although any fool could see that Tristan had issues with his family, it was also obvious that on some deep and primitive level he was also deeply bonded to them. *In my family you get…roots so deep they're like anchors of concrete, holding you so tightly that you can't move.*

That was how it was. How he was, and there was nothing anyone could do to change it. The question was, could they somehow find a way to live with it? As the car made its way through the narrow streets of the Barri Gotic she very tentatively reached out and covered his hand with hers.

'Tristan, I know I was wrong to—'

Very gently he moved his hand away and turned his head to face her. The streetlights shone on the rain-wet, night-black window, lining his face with watery shadows.

'No,' he said flatly. 'You weren't wrong. *I* was. I was

wrong to think this could be more than just a business arrangement, Lily. I was wrong to let you think it was ever going to work.'

Lily felt the blood drain from her face as his shocking, hurtful words sank in. 'But what about this afternoon?

'A mistake.'

'No...' she whimpered. 'Tristan, no.'

'Yes.' His voice was low and forceful. 'I'm thinking of you, Lily; I'm trying to do what's best for you. We have to keep up this charade in front of everyone else, but I can't do it all the time in private as well.' He sighed. 'From now on, it's as we discussed at the start. A business arrangement. A marriage in name only.'

Lily was too shocked to cry. She had gambled, and she had lost. Everything, including her dignity and her heart. All she had left was her baby.

That night Lily lay on her side of the wide bed that had been the scene of such rapturous lovemaking earlier. She felt as if she were balanced on the edge of some dark and fathomless abyss.

The next morning Tristan went to the office and Dimitri collected her from the hotel and took her to Tristan's apartment in the Eixample. Left by herself, she walked slowly around her new home, admiring the pale blond wooden floors, the sleekly efficient kitchen with its stainless steel surfaces and gleaming run of fitted units, the big windows that looked out over the city to the sea in the distance, and thought wistfully of the cluttered house in Primrose Hill.

She felt very alone. And very certain that, not only had her brief honeymoon ended, but so, effectively, had her marriage.

CHAPTER TEN

'LILY, my darling!'

The nicotine-soaked rasp of Lily's agent in London reached down the telephone line into the quiet of the Barcelona apartment like an echo from another planet.

'Now, don't hang up, angel—I'm not ringing to pressure you about work, I just want to know how you are. And of course make sure that you're eating properly and getting plenty of sleep, darling. I'm worried about you.'

'Just like the old days, Maggie,' said Lily with a smile as she sank down into one of Tristan's squat, modern sofas and slid a cushion into the small of her back. When Lily and Scarlet had arrived in London as green seventeen-year-olds Maggie Mason had clucked over them like a mother hen, although her motives were largely financial.

'Ah, the old days, when I had to beg clients to cast you because you always looked so shy and serious until you got in front of a camera. That *does* seem a long time ago. Now you're all grown up and married to the most eligible man in Europe! How's it going, darling?'

'Fine.' Lily heard the slight stiffness in her voice and forced herself to smile. 'I'm doing everything by the book. Tristan has registered me with the top obstetrician here, so I'm being well looked after.'

'That's good! Fantastic!' There was a pause, and Lily could vividly picture Maggie briskly tapping the ash from her cigarette into an ashtray placed precariously on the landslide of paper and magazines on her desk. 'Well, in that case, darling, how's everything else? You're keeping busy? Only you would not believe how inundated I am with requests for you to work. Simply swamped with demands from just about every luxury brand imaginable, all wanting the new Marquesa de Montesa to represent them. Of course I tell them all that it's impossible—that you're absolutely off the circuit and far too busy with your gorgeous husband and your glamorous life to *work*, for heaven's sake… Am I right?'

Lily hesitated for a fraction of a second, before saying brightly, 'Yes, yes, that's right, very busy,' but the lie seemed to echo around the emptiness of Tristan's stark and beautiful apartment. She tried to soften it a little. 'It's the baby, really. I mean, I'm sure if you could see me now the only work you'd be offering me would be the back end of a cow in a butter commercial.'

Unconsciously while she'd been talking she found that she'd pushed up the cashmere jumper of Tristan's that she was wearing and was gently rubbing the flat of her hand over the neat mound of her bump. At almost six months pregnant she already felt huge, and although she was deeply relieved that the stage of morning sickness had passed she found it constantly surprising how the simplest tasks suddenly seemed overwhelmingly challenging.

Maggie was not to be deflected. 'Come, come now, darling. I saw that picture in *Hello!* of you and Tristan at some function last week. Pregnancy suits you—although,' she teased, 'I'm not sure it can be entirely responsible for the luminous glow in your cheeks…'

Lily felt her face grow warm. The reception had been held at one of the impossibly grand function rooms at the Banco Romero and had been a stilted affair with endless formal photographs, for which Lily had been expected to take her place at Tristan's side.

That was the reason for the glow in her cheeks, she thought miserably. Because for a few moments her husband had circled his arm around her waist and held her against him. Because just the feel of his body against hers in a room full of strangers was enough to turn her knees to water. Who, looking at those photographs of the Marqués de Montesa so close to his pregnant wife, would have guessed that that was the first time he had touched or held her in weeks?

Ten weeks, to be precise. Since the night that she had worn the Romero jewels.

'No, really,' Lily stammered now, 'I love being pregnant. I know it sounds mad, but I really do.' Her voice softened, and her hand stilled on the bump as a wave of primitive love washed through her. Tristan's coldness and distance were so much more bearable because she had the constant comfort of the child inside her, making its gentle, rippling, fishlike movements. 'It's like being under some astonishing enchantment. My body has taken on this amazing life of its own.'

'Oh, rats,' drawled Maggie. 'I was hoping I'd find you bored to tears and desperate to get back to work. You're still doing the next instalment of the perfume ad, I suppose—but that's not until after the baby's due, which is ages away.' Maggie paused, and Lily heard her take a deep drag of nicotine before she continued thoughtfully. 'I don't suppose you'd consider a lifestyle feature, just to keep the masses happy would you? Something along the lines of "my fairy-tale marriage to the gorgeous blue-blooded Spanish billionaire"?'

Lily suddenly felt very cold. 'No. No, I don't think that would be a good idea.'

'Darling, why not? You're so buried in domestic bliss that you're perhaps not aware that your fabulously romantic marriage has made you absolutely the hottest ticket in town. I've heard rumours about paparazzi photographers remortgaging their houses to pay for tip-offs about your antenatal appointments, and which parties you and Tristan will be appearing at. You can't buy this kind of publicity, so when it comes along, by God, you have to make the most of it...'

Lily's knuckles were white as she gripped the phone. 'No,

Maggie, and—oh, gosh—talking of antenatal appointments reminds me, I'm going to be late for one if I don't get a move on. Thanks so much for ringing. It's gorgeous to talk, and I'll phone you if I change my mind about work or anything.'

A little later as she sat behind the silent Dimitri on the way to her appointment at Dr Alvarez's office Lily thought back over the conversation. *My fairy-tale marriage to the gorgeous blue-blooded Spanish billionaire indeed.*

What a joke.

What would Maggie say if she knew that at this moment Lily didn't even know where the gorgeous blue-blooded Spanish billionaire was, or who he was with? He had left two days ago on one of his frequent 'business trips', as usual giving no clue as to when he would be back. And although in many ways his physical absence was easier to bear than the great yawning distance that he so carefully put between them when he was home, it still hurt.

How, she thought bleakly, had she ended up deceiving all the people she cared about most?

She was saved from coming up with the answer to that question by Dimitri's guttural voice with its impenetrable Russian accent.

'Nearly there, Marquesa. I park at front?'

'Yes, please, Dimitri.' She smiled ruefully. It made no difference how many times she told him to call her Lily. 'How is Irina?'

He didn't reply, but once the car had come to a standstill in front of Dr Alvarez's building he reached into his pocket for a creased piece of paper and handed it to her with a little grunt. It showed the grainy amphibian outline of his sister's unborn twins.

'Oh, Dimitri, look! They're adorable! And getting so big… When are they due?'

He had come round to open the car door for her. 'Six weeks. But maybe they come sooner.'

Lily gathered up her bag and prepared to ease her bulk out

of the car and Dimitri put a steady hand beneath her elbow. It made her smile to think that she'd mistaken the gentle giant for a gangster the night she'd arrived in Barcelona. It seemed so ridiculously naïve now. But then so did a lot of the things she'd thought back then.

'How is she?' Lily asked gently. Dimitri had told her that Irina had lost her husband and both of their families in a terrible bombing raid on their village. Dimitri had been trying to persuade her to come to Barcelona before the babies were born, but she was unwilling to leave the place that was her last link with her husband.

'Always tired. Her blood has not enough...' he frowned '...metal?'

'Iron,' said Lily. 'Are they looking after her all right?'

Dimitri nodded, implacable behind his dark glasses. 'Señor Romero make sure. He pay for best doctors. He look after her.'

How typical of Tristan, thought Lily as she made her way slowly up the steps to Dr Alvarez's consulting rooms. Dutiful to the last—even to the unknown sister of his driver, thousands of miles away in Russia. She hated the mean little part of her that resented the idea of Tristan looking after anyone else. But she had so little of him, so very, very little, that it hurt to know that she shared those dry crumbs with anyone else.

Sighing, Lily paused at the top of the steps and took the mobile phone from her bag and dialled his number. Waiting for him to answer, she pictured him sprawled across the bed in some lavish hotel, a sultry beauty lying with her head on her chest, her dark hair spilling over the rumpled sheets. As the ringing continued she imagined him reluctantly disentangling himself from the long, tanned limbs of the beautiful woman and cursing quietly as he searched through the pile of hastily discarded clothes on the floor for his mobile...

'Hello?'

Lily's heart rocketed as his voice reached her ear; dark, rich, husky. She felt the heat flood her face. Her face, and her body.

'Tristan, it's me. Lily.'

'I know.'

'Oh, yes. Yes, of course.' She closed her eyes, willing the surge of stupefying need that just hearing his voice had aroused to subside again. 'Look, I've just arrived at Dr Alvarez's office for my scan. He has this high-tech equipment that means that you can see it on the Internet...' She felt her throat tighten. 'I just thought...if you're anywhere near a computer...'

There was a long pause.

'Tristan? Are you still there?'

'Yes.' She thought she heard him sigh, but it could have been static on the line. 'I'll connect my laptop now.'

It sounded so easy, Tristan thought as he switched on the computer and waited to see if there was any chance that the wireless connection was going to play ball today. The things that people took so much for granted in the modern world, like electricity or phone signals, were erratic and unreliable in Khazakismir, which was almost more difficult to deal with than if they hadn't been available at all.

The health centre's small office was currently doubling up as a storeroom to house the massive influx of basic medicinal supplies that Tristan had demanded on the day of the village raid all those months ago, meaning the desk was pushed right up against the window in the corner. Since that time things had been quieter here, and the rhythm of day-to-day life—never smooth or easy—had gradually been restored, giving them a chance to finish off the building and recruit and train some more staff from the local population. The health centre was still full, still struggling to cope, but the cases they were dealing with were the effects of the harsh winter and poor nutrition; influenza, pneumonia, sheer exhaustion from the grinding stress of living in poverty, rather than the bloody aftermath of deliberate violence. Today the cries that echoed through the corridors were not those of the maimed and bereaved, but of a woman giving birth.

Things were running fairly smoothly now, and the staff Tristan employed via the charitable trust had proved to be competent and courageous beyond anything he could have hoped. He didn't need to be here at all.

And yet he kept coming back.

Kept running away.

Swearing softly, he stared at the screen of the small computer, until the little hourglass danced in front of his eyes. He remembered Lily telling him about the scan a while ago, and about the latest technology that enabled absent fathers to view their babies over an Internet connection, but he had pushed the information to the back of his mind.

Or maybe he hadn't.

Maybe that was why he had flown out here two days ago, on the private mental pretext of dealing with a missing consignment of supplies, which, if he was honest, was never likely to be recovered. Maybe it was because all the red tape and tightrope negotiations with volatile local government officials was easier than being at his wife's side and getting a first glimpse at his unborn child.

Straightening up he slammed his fist down on the desk, making the laptop bounce alarmingly. A second later the screen changed, signalling that the elusive Internet connection had finally been established.

From down the hallway the woman in labour gave a low cry, like an animal in pain. Tristan's mobile phone rang.

'Señor Romero? It's Dr Alvarez's secretary. Are you ready to be put through to the scan room?'

For a moment there was nothing to be seen but a grainy moonscape of grey, broken by a paler crescent of white. Tristan straightened up and exhaled, realising only then that he had been holding his breath, mentally bracing himself against whatever he might see. But this he could deal with. The screen in front of him showed a picture like television static, a tiny white arrow racing across meaningless ghostly shapes in the snowstorm, clicking and measuring.

Measuring what? His chest lurched as he wondered if, whatever they were, the measurements were OK.

And then suddenly the screen split, and on the right hand side another window opened up onto a sepia-toned underwater world. For a moment Tristan wasn't sure what he was looking at as the sonogram moved around and the image swirled and billowed, but then the screen stilled and the picture resolved itself, and he was looking at his baby's face.

It was astonishingly clear, astonishingly *real*. The baby was in half profile, its eyes closed, a tiny, perfect hand pressed against one rounded cheek. As he watched a frown flickered across its face and the hand moved, the delicate fingers stretching and uncurling like fronds of coral as the baby opened its rosebud mouth wide and gave a restless movement of its head, as if it were looking for something. And then a second later it stilled again as the thumb of the small, flailing hand found its place in the tiny mouth.

Tristan was dimly aware of the ache in his back, but it was only when the screen flickered and went blank that he realised he had half risen to his feet and was leaning forward, gripping the edge of the desk, every muscle taut as wire. He straightened up, blinking fast, balling his hands into fists as the blood returned to his fingers and the drumming in his ears subsided.

He felt dizzy, as if the weight of the responsibility he had been keeping so distant had suddenly come crashing down on him, crushing him. The walls of the small, cluttered office seemed to inch inwards, closing in on him and he looked around wildly at the stacks of boxes and files of paperwork and the whiteboards on the walls filled with scrawled updates about roadside patrols and rebel movements.

None of it made sense.

He had thrown himself into this project, ploughing money, time, energy into it under some ridiculous illusion that he was being completely altruistic. His way of putting back some of the wealth his family had taken from those who needed it most over the years. His way of making amends, living with himself, sleeping at night. He had taken on despotic dictators, violent warlords, disease and hunger simply to avoid having to confront the real things in his life. The things that *really* scared him.

That he might not be a good father. That if he got close he would pass on the legacy of his father to his child. But as he snatched up the laptop and shrugged into his coat Tristan knew that it wasn't the weight of responsibility he could feel pressing the air from his lungs, or fear that was making his heart pound.

How stupid of him not to have realised earlier that it was love.

'The heartbeat is just a little accelerated, but it's nothing to worry about. Probably the *bambino's* excitement at being on camera. Go home and take it easy. Get an early night, and, above all, don't worry.'

That was easier said than done, Lily thought as she lay down her book with a sigh. She had followed the rest of Dr Alvarez's advice to the letter, and being in bed at just after nine o'clock was a record even for her, but the not worrying had proved impossible. Rearranging the bank of pillows behind her, she sighed and turned out the light.

Dr Alvarez's words seemed to echo a little more loudly, a little more ominously in the darkness of the silent apartment. *The heartbeat is just a little accelerated…* He had looked worried when he'd said that, hadn't he?

She switched the light back on and sat up.

'I'm being silly,' she said aloud, her voice cracking slightly from not having spoken to anyone since she'd left the surgery all those hours ago. 'Auntie Scarlet would say I need to get out more.'

She hadn't spoken to anyone *visible*, she amended with a rueful smile as she wearily got out of bed and padded into the kitchen to make a cup of chamomile tea. Talking to the baby was something she did automatically; naturally. Sometimes she wondered if it was normal. Mostly she didn't care. She had to talk to someone.

Anyway, who was to say what was normal any more?

In the kitchen she poured boiling water onto a teabag to produce something that looked and smelled like pondwater. She felt a tug of pain, deep inside her. Normal would be having a husband here to bring her tea in bed, rub her back, tell her she was worrying about nothing. Normal would be being able to phone him, just to hear his voice, just to share her concerns and have him reassure her...

She got back into bed and looked wistfully at the phone for a second, her fingers tingling with the overwhelming urge to pick it up and dial his number. She wanted to talk to him, to ask him if he'd been able to see the scan pictures. What had he thought? Had he been as blown away by them as she had?

The ache inside her intensified as the unwelcome answer to that question presented itself in her head. Turning out the light, she curled up, pulling her knees up tight against her and feeling the baby press against her thighs.

She sighed.

'Goodnight, little one,' she said sadly. 'I love you.'

She was woken by a tearing pain that seemed to grip her whole body, making it feel as if huge, cruel hands were grasping at her flesh, twisting it without mercy. For a mute, horror-struck moment she didn't move as doors in her mind seemed to clang shut, trying to close out the terrible, nightmarish truth.

But it was like trying to hold back the sea. It burst in, smashing the light from her world.

'No, no, no...' She was saying it out loud, her voice rising in a crescendo of screaming panic as she struggled from the bed and tried to stand up.

Her legs buckled beneath her and she fell to the floor, still clutching at the duvet. It slithered off the bed to show sheets that were red with blood.

CHAPTER ELEVEN

THE light filtering through the slats of the blind was thin and grey, but to Lily it felt as if someone were shining a spotlight on the inside of her skull. Squeezing her eyes tightly shut, she tried to turn over to face the other way, to shut it out for ever.

Ten thousand red-hot razor blades of pain bit into her, brutally dragging her back into consciousness, and jagged terror snagged in her brain.

Blood.

Blood everywhere. She remembered sticky warmth running down her legs…remembered putting her hand down to touch it, and the terrible jewel-bright redness on her fingers. Clumsily now she tried to lift her hand to see if she had dreamed it, but the movement sent a guillotine of pain slicing through her arm.

'Shh… Lie still.'

Tristan's face swam in front of her, grave and perfectly still, as if it had been carved in granite. Lily felt the pain recede a little as he brushed the hair back from her forehead and stroked his fingers down her cheek. He was here, and the sheer strength of his presence soothed her. Whatever had happened, Tristan could make it all right again.

With his hand still warm against her cheek, Lily let herself be pulled back down into blissful oblivion.

So this was his punishment.

Tristan felt the ache of exhaustion bite into his bones and

scream along the muscles and nerves of his arm. Lily was asleep again now, her exquisite face as pale as milk from all the blood she had lost, but still he forced himself to go on stroking her hair, her cheek. As a gesture of comfort it was so pitifully small, so very inadequate, but it was all he could do.

All he could bloody well do.

He had promised to protect her, to keep her safe and he'd failed. Spectacularly. He had offered her *security*, and thought that that was nothing more than a luxurious home. A *name*.

And in the end that name had counted for nothing. A title and a bloodline and all the Romero riches hadn't kept their baby safe, because the only thing that could have done that was Tristan himself.

And he wasn't there.

A baby girl, the doctor had told him. His jaw set like steel and he kept his eyes fixed unblinkingly ahead, refusing to look down at the fragile figure in the bed. Her peacefulness was like a deliberate reproach, because he knew that soon he would have to shatter it when he tried to explain to her just what she had lost. Outside a watery winter dawn was breaking over Barcelona, filtering into the room through the slats of the blind. They seemed to Tristan like bars of a prison.

A prison of guilt, in which he would serve a life sentence.

'You're here.'

Her voice was a whisper—barely more than a breath—but it made Tristan jump just as if she'd shouted. He forced himself to look down at her, but suddenly found that his throat had closed around and he couldn't speak. *Yes, I'm here. Where I should have been all along.*

He nodded.

'I thought I'd dreamed it earlier,' she said softly.

'No. You didn't dream it. I'm here.'

'That's good, but...' Her eyelashes fluttered down over her cheeks for a moment and her brows drew together in a frown. When she looked back up at him her eyes were clouded with anxiety. 'But that means I didn't dream the rest either, doesn't it?'

'Yes. I'm afraid so.'

Her face was ashen and she spoke through bloodless lips. 'What happened?'

Tristan stood up abruptly, turning his back on her and going over to the window. It was early afternoon, and a pale winter sun had broken through the leaden clouds and was now making the wet city streets gleam like polished silver. Finding the words, speaking them without breaking down, was going to be the hardest thing he had ever done, but he had to be strong for her.

He had done so little else, after all.

'It was something called a...' He stopped, ruthlessly slashing back the emotion that threatened to crack his voice. '...a placental abruption. That's what caused the bleeding. By the time I found you, you had lost a lot of blood, and the baby...'

He squeezed his eyes very tightly shut for a second, as if that could dispel the image of what he had found when he'd finally let himself into the apartment late last night. But there was a part of him that knew already that it would always be there in his head, a lifelong reminder of his culpability. Savagely he thrust his clenched fists into his pockets and turned around. *Dios*, he had to at least look at her when he said this.

'The baby had died already.'

The only movement she made was to close her eyes. Apart from two small lines between her fine brows her paper-white face was completely composed, so that for a moment he thought she might have slipped back into her morphine-induced slumber. And then he saw that tears were running down her cheeks and into her hair in a steady, glistening river.

He stood, stony and utterly helpless in the face of her silent, dignified suffering. Slowly he approached the bed and sat down beside her again, picking up her hand from the sheet. It felt cold, and his chest contracted painfully as he looked down and saw how very pale and fragile her fingers looked against his.

'I'm sorry.' His voice was a low, hoarse rasp.

Almost imperceptibly she nodded, but her eyes stayed closed, shutting him out of her private grief. It was hardly surprising, he thought bitterly. It was his fault. How on earth could he expect her to forgive him when he would never be able to forgive himself?

Especially when she eventually found out the rest, and understood the devastating extent of her loss: that by the time he had found her she had lost too much blood, and they hadn't been able to stop it coming and had had to operate to remove her womb...

That she had not only lost this baby, but any chance she might have had of having any more.

Because he hadn't been there.

After a few more minutes he got up and very quietly left the room. She didn't open her eyes, so she never saw the tears that were running down his face.

Steadily the room filled up with flowers, exotic fleshy blooms sent by Scarlet and Tom and Maggie and the cosmetics company and all the crew from the perfume advertisement shoot, which made the air turn heavy with their intoxicating hot-house scent. Nurses came and went, some silent and compassionate, some brisk and matter-of-fact. Lily was indifferent to them all.

She felt hollowed out and as insubstantial as air. All the feelings that had nagged at her before that fateful night at Stowell—of emptiness and futility—came back now; swollen to huge and grotesque proportions, ballooning inside her until there was no space for anything else.

Which was good, she thought distantly, watching a nurse change the bag of fluid that had been dripping into her arm, because at least it stopped her from thinking about Tristan. Longing for him.

She wondered where he was; if he had gone back to wherever he had been once he had broken the news about the baby. The image of his set, emotionless face as he told her what had happened kept coming back to her, and the carefully controlled way he'd said, 'I'm sorry.'

It must have been hard for him, she recognised that. So hard for him to keep his relief from showing, but typical of him to try so dutifully.

The nurse smiled kindly, folding back the heavy hospital blankets to check the dressing covering Lily's scar. 'Your husband rang, *señora*,' she said in her cheerful, sing-song Catalan. 'To ask how you are and to see if he might come back to see you this afternoon?'

Lily turned her head away, biting her lip as several explanations for Tristan's desire to see her flashed into her brain; none of them good.

'I… I'm not sure…I…'

She looked down. The nurse had peeled back the gauze dressing to show the livid scar that cut across her pitifully flat stomach. Lily felt her insides turn cold with horror, everything in her recoiling from the square of torn and deflated flesh and what it meant.

The nurse seemed pleased.

'Healing nicely,' she said with a complacent smile, dabbing iodine onto Lily's skin as if she were glazing pastry. 'You will be able to go home in no time.'

Lily moistened her cracked lips with her tongue. 'But will it happen again? Next time?'

The nurse seemed to freeze for a moment, and then several different expressions crossed her face in quick succession: shock, pity, fear—and finally, as the doctor appeared in the doorway, relief.

'The doctor will explain everything.' She patted Lily's hand, hastily gathered up her tray of equipment and bustled towards the door.

When she went back later, she found Lily curled up into a foetal position, her face turned to the wall. Thinking she was asleep, the nurse was just about to tiptoe out again when Lily said, 'I'd like you to telephone Señor Romero and tell him not to come. Today, or any day.'

'Ah, *bambino*...' The nurse crossed to the bed in a rustle of starch and compassion and touched Lily's shoulder. 'Do not say that... A husband and wife must stick together in such terrible times. That is what marriage is for; for love and support...'

Slowly Lily turned over, and the expression on her face shocked the cheerful nurse into silence. Later she described it to her colleague on the ward as like an animal who knew it was dying and wanted to be left alone to do it.

'Not my marriage,' she said dully. 'My marriage is over now. There is nothing between us any more. Please tell him.'

There was a primal, ferocious glitter in her eyes as she spoke. Nodding mutely, the nurse bolted from the room.

CHAPTER TWELVE

Stowell, England. August.

'DEARLY beloved, we are gathered here in the sight of God to witness the marriage of Scarlet to Tom...'

Lily stared fixedly down at her ringless hands, clasped so tightly together on her knee that the knuckles gleamed, opal-white against the flowered silk of her dress.

'God and the world's media,' muttered Scarlet's brother Jamie beside her as the drone of helicopters circling the cloudless blue sky outside threatened to drown out the thin voice of the vicar. Lily managed a smile. The small church at Stowell was packed to the gills, and, while she would much rather have slipped anonymously into a back pew, Scarlet had other ideas.

'I completely understand that you don't want to be a bridesmaid, honey,' she had said gently as the hairdresser had teased and smoothed her dark hair around the stunning Montague diamond tiara, 'but you're the closest thing I have to a sister and I want you there, right next to Mum and Dad and Jamie. They need all the support they can get against the full force of Tom's crowd, believe me.'

But both of them had known that it was Scarlet's family who would be doing the supporting. The day that Scarlet had been waiting and planning for for a whole year was going to test every ounce of the strength and fragile sense of acceptance that Lily had built up over the six difficult months since she left Barcelona. The fact that Scarlet and Tom had picked the anniversary of their engagement at the Stowell summer ball to get married was just one more blow for Lily to absorb on flesh that was already bruised and bleeding.

The organ swelled for the first hymn and the congregation got to their feet. Lily opened her hymn book, relieved to have something to look at. The words to the hymn were familiar enough that she didn't need to read them, but at least staring down at them offered a temporary respite from the effort of not looking at Tristan.

He was standing just a few feet away at the front of the church beside Tom, the two of them tall and romantic in their morning suits. Lily had allowed herself a brief glance at him when she had first taken her place in the pew the moment before Scarlet had begun her stately progress down the aisle, but just the sight of his broad shoulders, the tanned hand he laid on Tom's arm in a brief gesture of support, had impaled her on a shaft of pure, intense pain.

"'Love divine, all loves excelling,'" sang the congregation. The printed words danced in front of Lily's eyes and her empty body wrenched with loneliness and misery. With massive effort she averted her thoughts, focusing instead on the enormous arrangement of tumbling flowers just in front of her. In the last six months she had become pretty expert in the art of refocusing, of training her mind to steer away from the danger areas, and she was proud of the progress she'd made. After the first terrible month when she'd returned to London and shut herself into the house in Primrose Hill and cried herself dry, gradually she had felt herself coming back to life.

Not the life she wanted and not the life she had had before. A new life.

"'Visit us with thy salvation. Enter every trembling heart…'"

Maggie had continued to try to tempt her with offers of work, but Lily knew that her modelling days were behind her.

Externally her scars had healed—the exhausted emergency doctor who had received her from the ambulance in the small hours of the morning had done a great job—and to the outside world she looked almost the same. But inside she had changed.

She felt blank. Scoured out. Sterile. A clean slate waiting for a new start.

The hymn ended and the congregation sat down gratefully, fanning themselves with service sheets in the August heat. At the altar, Scarlet and Tom stood shoulder to shoulder preparing to bind their lives together as the sun poured through the magnificent stained glass window above them, raining jewelled drops onto Scarlet's shimmering satin train. One of the many tiny bridesmaids recruited from the ranks of Tom's millions of cousins was steadily picking flowers out of her tightly bound bouquet and dropping them on the floor, and Lily closed her eyes as an image of the unknown little girl who had acted as her impromptu bridesmaid in the church in Barcelona came back to her.

She felt a smile steal across her lips, remembering how cross she'd been at the time at the hurried and unceremonious wedding Tristan had arranged. Now, looking back, all she could think of was how perfect it was. No pageantry, no theatre, just the beautiful church, empty and dark in the autumn evening, a few strangers whose lives had touched hers for a brief, significant moment, the sparse service, stripped back to its simplest form...

Tom's 'I will' was drowned out by a sudden wail as the small bridesmaid's bouquet disintegrated entirely, scattering flowers everywhere. Then an audible sigh of pleasure went up from the female members of the congregation as the strikingly handsome best man stepped forward and took her by the hand, bending to scoop up her fallen roses and giving them back to her.

Lily felt as if nails were being driven into her heart.

He looked thinner, she thought in anguish, the hollows beneath his cheekbones more pronounced. His brows were pulled down severely, which somehow made the tenderness of his actions all the more affecting.

It was no use, she thought despairingly. No matter how much she tried to avert her thoughts and her eyes, no matter how much she filled her days with activity or her head with new ideas, the truth was stamped on every cell of her body and in every beat of her heart. She lifted her head and looked to the front of the church, where everything she had ever wanted was symbolised before her.

Tristan, holding the hand of a little girl.

It should have been *her* husband, *her* child. The empty spaces inside her head seemed to stretch and darken as the grief that still stalked her crept a little closer again, but she gritted her teeth and pushed it back. She had something to hold onto now...a plan to focus on that had come to feel like a sort of lifeline over the past few weeks.

She just had to hope that he would help her.

The child's hand in his felt very small and soft, but her grip was surprisingly strong. Tristan loosened his own fingers in the hope that she would let go. Instead she seemed to hold on even more tightly.

Typical female, he thought with a sardonic twitch of his lips. He had stepped forward and taken hold of her hand completely instinctively, thinking only of heading off the storm of weeping that he could see had been just about to disrupt the whole service. Now he was beginning to regret the impulse. It appeared to be programmed into all women's DNA to cling on more tightly when they sensed you wanted to distance yourself from them.

No. Not all women...

A great weariness descended on him as the persistent whisper in his head tauntingly reminded him of the woman who had proved to be the exception to that and every other rule. Lily had never clung to him, in any way. Not throughout the brief weeks of their doomed marriage, when she had conducted herself with nothing but dignity in the face of his appalling coldness. Not at any stage of her pregnancy, when she had been tired or sick or worried, and not even at the end, when he had so badly wanted her to.

Dios, she hadn't even bothered with goodbye—not personally anyway, although he expected the one he had got via the kindly nurse was a lot more gentle and sympathetic than hers would have been.

'To have and to hold from this day forward...'

From across the aisle he was aware of Tatiana, one of Scarlet's modelling friends who was filling Lily's role of chief bridesmaid, eyeing him seductively from under her coronet of flowers. Deliberately he looked away, focusing his attention on the bride and groom. Tom was holding Scarlet's hand, looking straight into her eyes as he made his vows. His voice cracked with emotion, and Tristan gave a twisted smile. Tom had always been way too sensitive and sentimental—which had been why Tristan was constantly having to stop people beating him up at school.

'For better, for worse...in sickness and in health...'

The smile vanished and he couldn't stop the memory of another church, another wedding from stealing into the back of his mind. Another bride, in jeans and boots, her face bare of make-up and her hair tumbling down about her shoulders like a veil of spun gold.

The little bridesmaid's small hand felt as if it were burning his, and suddenly he wanted to walk away from it all—from the palpable love between the man and woman standing in front of him, from the child holding his hand, from the mass of people grouped behind him, amongst which was Lily...

Tom said that since she'd come back to London she was doing OK. She was coping, beginning to pick up the pieces and move on. He had also added with uncharacteristic vehemence that if Tristan did or said *anything* to upset her today he would never forgive him. Scarlet had suggested he just stayed well out of her way.

'As long as we both shall live.'

She was probably right. Wouldn't anything he could say just sound insultingly inadequate? Grinding his teeth together, Tristan stared straight ahead, concentrating on a memorial stone set into the wall right in front of him. *Edmund Montague, fourth Earl of Cotebrook,* he read quickly, as if by filling his brain with facts he could hold back the tide of emotion that he could sense rising all around him, threatening to breach the defences of a lifetime, *Officer in the King's Regiment...Loving husband and devoted father...*

And as Tom drew back the veil from his bride's face and kissed her lingeringly, and the congregation—mainly on Scarlet's side—burst into a round of spontaneous applause, Tristan extricated himself from the warm grasp of the small girl beside him and stood alone.

Alone with his failings.

In all of its seven-hundred-year history, surely Stowell Castle had never looked lovelier than it did that afternoon, reclining gently in its rolling fields of yellow and green, the flags flying from the turrets almost motionless against a sky of flawless blue.

Jamie appeared at Lily's side with two glasses of champagne. 'It's far too hot for this ridiculous get-up,' he complained, looking at Lily's bare arms with envy. 'How soon can I take off my jacket and this tie thing, do you think?'

Lily gave him a sympathetic look. 'I think etiquette would say not until Tom does.'

Jamie groaned, and gave his cravat a vicious tug. 'Do you think blue blood is a bit colder than normal blood? Like reptiles?'

Lily had just leaned forward to straighten Jamie's tie when a shadow fell across them and the bright afternoon seemed to darken. She looked up and felt the breath stop in her throat. This was the moment she'd been dreading, the moment she'd been hoping and wishing and waiting for for the last three months.

Her fingers froze, clutching the silk of Jamie's cravat, and her heart hammered crazily against her ribs as she looked up into Tristan's face.

It was like an Arctic wind in the heat of the soft English afternoon.

'I think you could be right.' She stepped back, dropping her gaze. 'Jamie, have you met Tom's best man, Tristan Romero? Tristan, this is Jamie Thomas.'

Jamie looked at Tristan and then back at Lily, his mouth opening as realisation dawned.

'Tom's…Oh. Right,' said Jamie awkwardly, clearly wondering whether he should bow in deference to Tristan's title, apologise for the reptile comment, or punch him for walking out on his sister's best friend. 'Well, I was just going to get another drink, so…'

Jamie melted away. And as far as Lily was concerned so did the other guests, the rose-garlanded marquee, the waiters with their trays of vintage champagne, the castle, the lake, the rest of the world. As she stood a few feet away from Tristan, looking into his eyes, nothing else existed but themselves and the history that no one else understood. For a moment, a wonderful, terrible, wrenching moment, Lily thought she saw the pain she carried around secretly inside herself reflected in the intense blue of his eyes.

And then he looked away and the moment was gone.

'How are you, Lily?' he said. Courteous, civilised, *dutiful*.

Of course.

'I'm fine.'

A lie, but an excusable one. One told with the best of intentions—to save him awkwardness, to protect herself, to make him more likely to consider the question she needed to ask him. And besides, in a relationship built on half-truths and evasions, what difference did one more small deceit make?

'Good. I'm glad. You're looking…' he paused, a frown

flickering over his face as his gaze swept over her '…as beautiful as ever.'

So he was clearly not averse to lying either. Lily gave a small, painful smile. The connection she thought she had felt a moment ago had completely vanished now and a bleak, frozen continent of unspoken misery lay between them.

'Thank you,' she said ruefully. 'I appreciate your dishonesty. I wish my agent was as good at lying as you are.'

With narrowed eyes Tristan looked out into the distance, away from her. His voice was distant too. Polite.

'You're not working?'

She shook her head, holding onto her champagne glass with both hands to keep it steady. 'Not since the last perfume commercial.' She laughed. 'And after that disaster I probably won't work again.'

'What happened?'

'It was the follow up to the wedding one we shot in…in Rome that day.' *Our wedding day.* 'It was the next instalment in the story.'

'Let me guess,' he said gruffly. 'A baby?'

She nodded. 'I don't think the director or the crew were terribly impressed with my lack of professionalism.'

'*Dios*, Lily—'

'It doesn't matter,' she said quickly, desperately trying to withstand the annihilating wave of longing that smashed through her as she heard the slight rasp of emotion behind his words. She took a swift mouthful of champagne. 'I never wanted to be a model anyway. It was something I fell into and I kept on doing it because there was no reason not to. But in the last year everything has changed.'

They both found themselves looking down towards the lake. Tristan felt as if he were tied to a railway track and the train were getting closer. He nodded.

'Dimitri's sister,' she said quietly. 'I often think about her. Did she have her twins?'

'Yes. A boy and a girl. Emilia and Andrei.'

She exhaled slowly; a mixture of joy and anguish. 'Ah. How lovely...'

Tristan's head jerked round. 'Lily...'

'No, really, it's fine. I'm thrilled for her. I have to get over what happened...move on,' she said more wistfully. 'I want to move out of London, try to do something useful. The original charity who asked me to be an ambassador in Africa aren't keen to proceed at the moment because...because of what happened. They don't feel I could cope with seeing children suffering just yet, and they're probably right, but I'm looking into other ways I can be useful to them, and—'

She stopped, aware that she was talking faster and faster in her desperation to get to the point, and finding that now she had she didn't know what to say. Her head throbbed with dread and hope.

'Tristan, there's something else. Something I need your help with.'

He turned back, looking at her blankly. 'Money? If you're not working, I'd be happy to help out. We are still married, after all.'

'No. It's not that.' She took a deep breath. 'Not the money anyway, although the being married part is relevant, I suppose. You see, I want to try to adopt a child. I know it's very soon after...we lost our daughter...but I feel, deep down, that it's something I profoundly want to do. I just can't imagine...the rest of my life...without...'

She was breathing hard, unevenly, trying to hold the tears back. Trying to ignore the voice in her head that whispered, *You. I can't imagine the rest of my life without children and you...*

He stood very still, his inscrutable face giving nothing away. 'How can I help?' he said tonelessly. 'Can you do this privately? Can I pay?'

She shook her head. 'Unfortunately even the Romero billions can't buy what I want,' she said ruefully. 'There's a process—a long, difficult process to go through with social workers and being vetted for suitability, and approval is by no means certain. I don't want to get turned down. This is my last, my only chance. I want to make sure this happens for me, Tristan.'

A muscle ticced in his cheek. 'What do you want of me?'

'I want us to apply together. I think the chances of success will be greater if I'm part of a couple than if I apply by myself—an ex-model from a single parent family with a broken marriage behind her doesn't look good. I know our marriage was something you never wanted, and neither did I, but I did it for you. And now I'm asking you to do this for me.'

'Do what exactly?'

'Continue the pretence that we're a normal married couple…' there was a hard, cold edge to her voice now '…very much in love. It won't be easy, but of course privately we can go on as before. You can live your life, have your freedom and I won't ask any questions. And then at the end of it we go our separate ways.'

Very slowly he shook his head. 'It's impossible.'

'Tristan, don't say that—'

'Lily, you must know that it is,' he said despairingly. 'We tried it before and it nearly destroyed us both. Living a lie like that, pretending out of some sense of obligation or duty—I can't do it again.'

A sheet of ice formed itself instantly over Lily's heart. She felt the blood leave her face. *It wasn't a lie for me,* she wanted to shout. *I wasn't pretending to love you.* Light-headed, cold with horror, she began to back away as Tristan's face blurred behind a veil of humiliating tears.

'OK. I understand…' she gasped, holding up her hands in front of her as he opened his mouth to protest.

'Lily, wait!' he growled. 'Just listen—'

But at that moment an arm slid round her shoulders and she looked up to see Jamie had appeared beside her. He was looking at Tristan with unconcealed dislike.

'They're waiting for you to start the receiving line,' he said coldly. 'Although I think that Lily can be excused that ordeal.'

He turned his attention to her, his face softening with concern.
'Are you all right?'

She nodded, closing her eyes against the tears.

When she opened them again Tristan was gone.

CHAPTER THIRTEEN

HELL, thy name is wedding reception.

Sitting at the top table in the sweltering afternoon heat, Tristan gritted his teeth and looked at his still-full champagne glass. He felt as if he were the victim of some sadistic, protracted torture technique designed to test his strength and endurance and will power in every way possible.

The wedding breakfast was over, and as the guests dozed over coffee Scarlet's father turned over yet another page of his speech. Beside Tristan, Tatiana's slim thigh, encased in duck-egg blue silk, pressed against his.

There had been a time when his automatic response to any kind of emotion would have been to obliterate it with some hot, meaningless, commitment-free sex, and back in those days the sultry looks coming his way from the chief bridesmaid would have been extremely good news.

He moved away slightly.

Unfortunately for Tatiana it had been a long time since he had dealt with things that way. A year, to be precise. And as a strategy for emotional avoidance it had to be said that particular night had backfired spectacularly.

Automatically his hand moved across the table and his fingers closed around the stem of his glass, twisting it round while he resisted the temptation to pick it up and drain it. He badly wanted something to take the edge off the torment, and in the absence of a revolver and a single bullet alcohol seemed to offer his best chance, but unfortunately he had to stand up and make a speech in a minute.

Or perhaps that was being optimistic, he thought sourly. If Scarlet's father continued at his present rate Tristan would have plenty of time to down a bottle and sober up again before it was his turn.

If he leaned forward he could just see Lily's profile, half hidden by Jamie Thomas's lean frame. The razor wire wrapped around Tristan's heart tightened a little and his chest burned with the effort of not getting up, vaulting across the table and snatching her up into his arms.

Dios. Dios mio... Why hadn't she given him a chance to finish?

Finally Mr Thomas brought his speech to a close and everyone rose to their feet and toasted the bride and groom with enthusiastic relief. Tristan's hand was like a vice around his glass as he put it to his lips, wondering whether to take this chance to grab Lily and slip out. His head buzzed with the need to talk to her.

Too late. Tom was already getting to his feet as everyone else settled down into their seats once again. Tristan, caged and crucified by his own moral code of courtesy and duty, sat down too, clenching his hands together and resting his forehead on them as Tom started to speak.

'Ladies and gentlemen...I'll make this brief.'

Not bloody brief enough, thought Tristan dully, his heart jerking violently against his ribs as he looked at Lily. Not brief enough.

Tom was as good as his word. His speech was short and typically full of wry, self-deprecating humour and as the guests rose to their feet again to toast the bridesmaids they were still smiling.

The vintage champagne burned Lily's throat like acid as she choked back sudden tears and stared out of the marquee into the melting, strawberry-sorbet sunset. It was nearly over now, she told herself desperately. She only had to hold it together for a little bit longer before she could slip away quietly and howl out her sorrow and frustration and emptiness into the goosedown pillows of her room.

Tristan's refusal earlier had felt like another loss. Not of a real child this time, but of hope. Of another little bit of her future. She wasn't sure how much more loss she could take.

It would be so much easier if she could hate him, she thought bleakly, absent-mindedly twirling a sugar flower from the top of the wedding cake between her fingers. She *should* hate him: this was the man who had delivered the news of their baby's death in flat, emotionless tones, and then left her alone in the hospital. The same man who had just crushed her fragile dream with a single word.

But then she would remember the pain she sometimes glimpsed beneath the layer of ice in his eyes, the mask of honour and duty she suspected he wore to cover up the loneliness of his upbringing. She remembered the torment on his face sometimes when sleep had stripped away that mask, and she knew that it was hopeless. He touched her in places she couldn't help responding to, regardless of how sensible that response was, or how healthy. She hadn't chosen to fall in love with him, just as she hadn't chosen anything else that had happened to her in the last year, but now it had happened she had to live with it. Minimise the damage.

Around her she felt a frisson of interest stir the syrupy afternoon air. The girls on her table—a mixture of heiresses and models—were all sitting up a little straighter, fluffing up hair that had been flattened earlier beneath extravagant hats. Looking up, Lily immediately saw why.

At the top table Tristan had got to his feet.

Lily had the sensation of being in a lift as it plunged quickly downwards. He was so golden and gorgeous, but as she looked up at him she recognised a new severity in his features that she hadn't seen before. The intense blue eyes were the same, and the perfect cheekbones and the square chin with its deeply carved cleft, but, indefinably, gone was any trace of that louche, wicked playboy who had stepped out of the helicopter last summer and kissed her so audaciously. Looking away quickly, she saw that the sugar flower had crumbled to dust in her fingers.

'As a Spaniard this role of 'best man' is not one I'm very familiar with...' Tristan began, and a little sigh of female appreciation went round the marquee as that deep, husky Spanish voice filled the evening. Gazing out across the lawns, Lily felt it shiver across her skin, spreading goosebumps of longing as her poor, ravaged body stirred with feelings she had suppressed for a long time and her head was filled with a picture of a dark church, a handful of people.

'And when Tom asked me to do it I initially refused on the grounds that he's clearly a far better man than I am,' Tristan went on. A ripple of laughter greeted this. He had them all in the palm of his hand, thought Lily painfully. It was completely impossible to remain immune to that combination of grave intelligence and those killer good looks.

'However, when he sent me a copy of a book called *The Complete Guide to Being a Best Man* I discovered that it was not so much a competitive event as a series of clearly defined duties.'

More laughter.

Duties. Lily closed her eyes for a second against the pain.

'There are quite a lot of them,' he went on huskily, holding the book up and bending it back so that the pages flickered out like a fan, 'but I have learned recently that to do something out of *duty* is not always the best approach...'

Every word was another turn of the screw. Wasn't it enough that he had shattered her last hope, she thought numbly, without making her suffer so publicly too?

Tristan gave Tom a lopsided smile and put the book down on the table. 'Thanks for the thought, Tom, but I'm going to do this my way.'

Outside beyond the silken drapes of the marquee, the blush-pink sun was dipping down behind the trees around the lake, staining the sky the same colour as the roses in Scarlet's bouquet. In the centre of the lake the tower stood, dark and forbidding, its windows reflecting the sinking crimson sun and making it look as if it were on fire. Tristan's voice, deep and grave, went on, talking about the perfection of the day. Lily's head was filled with a sort of roaring, as if she were standing on the top of a mountain in a high wind.

Wishful thinking.

'...everything a wedding should be...' Tristan's voice reached her as if from a great distance '...champagne and roses; beautiful dresses and beautiful bridesmaids...'

Back in the real world, all around her, people smiled fondly. But then they couldn't know that the perfect, proper wedding that the best man was describing was the opposite in every way of his own hasty, hole-in-the-corner one to a woman he didn't love.

'It's about friends and families and laughing and dancing and fun.'

He stopped, looking down for a moment, frowning as if he was wondering how to go on. Everyone waited. The dying sun cast everything in a soft, rosy glow, adding to the sense of enchantment.

'That's a wedding. A *marriage* is a different thing entirely.' His voice was soft now, and filled with a kind of weary resignation. 'A marriage is about sharing, talking, compromising. It's about being honest. Being *there*.'

Enough.

Lily's throat burned and her eyes felt as if they were full of splinters as she got up and slipped quietly out from her place at the table. She walked quickly away from the marquee across the grass. The dew was falling and it was damp underfoot, making her heels sink into the soft ground so she paused for a second to kick them off and gather them up before stumbling onwards, blinded by tears. Tristan's voice followed her, filling her head and seeming to wrap itself around her in the velvety air, in a ceaseless, caressing taunt.

'Lily…'

She jerked to a standstill for a second as she realised that he was behind her, that what he was saying was her name. Then she carried on, faster than before, almost running down the sloping lawn towards the lake.

'Leave me alone, Tristan. Go back to your rapturous audience. I think I've heard enough.'

'Have you? I don't think so.'

She did stop then, whirling round to face him, her face blazing with anger that she no longer had the strength or the inclination to hide. 'How could you?' she croaked, and the rawness in her voice was shocking in the perfect, rose-pink evening. 'How could you stand up there in front of all those people and say that stuff about sharing and talking and…and *compromise*, for God's sake? How could you say it in front of *me*?'

Her voice was rising to a shout and there were tears running down her face. Taking a step towards him, she raised her hands, clenching her fists and pounding them against his chest as the anger and the grief, sealed in for so long, came spilling out.

'I never asked anything of you, Tristan! I didn't ask to be your wife, I didn't ask to be taken to a country where I knew no one and left alone there for days on end while you went away…' She gave a wild laugh. 'God, I didn't even ask where you went to! I asked for *nothing* and that's *exactly* what I got!'

Still her fists flailed at him, raining blows on his chest and his arms that he had absorbed without flinching, but now he caught hold of her wrists and held them tightly. 'What do you want?' His voice was a low rasp, edged with despair. 'What do you want, Lily?'

She went suddenly still. Their faces were inches apart and she could smell the citrus scent of his skin. It brought back a rush of memories that sent heat flooding downwards through her stomach. Heat and wetness and need.

I want everything we nearly had and didn't.

I want the impossible.

I want you.

'I just want some…consideration,' she said hoarsely, ruthlessly stamping out the need and the longing, fighting to hang
onto the anger of a moment ago. 'I want to not have to listen to
you standing up there theorising about what makes a successful
marriage, when ours was nothing but misery and loneliness.'
Her voice cracked and she tried to hide it with an ironic, self-
mocking laugh. 'Stupid as it sounds now, I wanted all that stuff
that you mentioned—the sharing and the talking, but most of
all I wanted…our baby. I wanted our baby so much.'

The sob that escaped her was muffled by his mouth coming
down on hers as he gathered her into his arms and pulled her
into his body. Her tears ran over his fingers as he held her face
in a kiss that went on and on, fuelled by despair and rage and
sadness and guilt.

Guilt that after all that had happened, after the enormity of
what she had lost, Lily found herself wanting to forget, just
for a moment. To be the person she had been—full of love,
instead of empty and angry and hollowed out by grief. Her
hands tangled into his hair, gripping tightly, and their teeth
clashed as she kissed him back with the ferocity of her anger.
And then he was lifting her up, sweeping her into his arms and
carrying her across the lawn, his breath coming in harsh, shaky
gasps, his chest rising and falling as he held her against it.

She didn't look up, didn't tear her mouth from his for a
moment, but she knew where they were going. Even before she
felt his footsteps slow, or heard the clatter of his feet against the
wooden boards of the walkway, she knew where he was taking
her.

Her tattered heart cried out in the emptiness inside her as
he carried her back to the place where it had all started.

Back to the tower.

It was as if time had caught, taken a wrong turning, looped
back on itself.

Everything was as she remembered, exactly the same. The
dying light coming through the arched windows, the apricot

glow behind the trees, the sparse room with the bed at its centre, like a stage. Everything.

Except...

Themselves.

The slow, dreamy languor with which they had touched each other last year was gone now, replaced by a desperation that made their movements swift and clumsy. Tristan didn't take her straight to the bed. Kicking the door shut, he let her slide from his arms and she slammed herself back against it, pulling him into her with a savagery that made him gasp.

'Lily...'

She didn't want gentle.

She couldn't do tender.

Gentleness had died in her along with her baby. Tenderness had been ripped out of her by the surgeons afterwards. Now she wanted oblivion.

'No,' she said harshly, grasping handfuls of his shirt and bunching it into her fists. 'No words. You don't have to worry, Tristan, I don't want love or tenderness or a happy ever after any more. Just make me forget, all right?'

Her voice was as jagged and cruel as broken glass, her movements swift and vicious. Her hips arched up towards his, grinding against the hardness of his arousal as her hands grappled with the buttons of his shirt until impatience got the better of her and she tore it open, exposing his bare chest to her fingernails, raking the flesh as he pushed up her skirt and tugged at her knickers, tearing the silk before entering her with a single powerful thrust that made her cry out in fierce triumph.

He drove into her with a relentlessness that made her dried and shrivelled heart sing, and with every hard push she felt the twin demons of anger and grief receding. Heat was spreading inside her, sending out bright tongues of flame to the furthest extremities of her body and building to a core of white brightness at a point in the cradle of her pelvis.

She closed her eyes, focusing on the light, and the movements of the muscles under his skin as she held onto his shoulders. He was carrying her, holding her and she was going to shatter...

She let go, crying out and throwing her head back so that it banged against the door, opening her eyes and looking at him through the fiery haze of sensation that claimed her.

And then she felt herself crashing down, spiralling back to earth.

Her heart stuttered and stopped and she felt the heat in her veins turn to ice. With a final shuddering thrust Tristan bent his head and hid his face in her hair, but not before she'd seen the expression of extreme suffering it bore.

They stood, motionless, still locked together as their breathing steadied. Staring into the melting remains of the day, Lily's eyes stung with tears she couldn't shed. Tristan's head was heavy on her shoulder. Then he seemed to gather himself, straightening up as if it hurt him. Wordlessly he picked her up and carried her to the bed.

Ecstasy and despair, balanced on a knife edge, she thought numbly. After the pleasure, the pain.

Except for him there had been no pleasure.

Duty.

That was all.

Always Duty.

The moment he placed her down on the bed, Lily rolled away, lying with her back to him and tucking her knees up against her body. Tristan felt the ever-present guilt harden inside him, mixing uneasily with self-loathing.

How could he have been so crass?

He had wanted her so badly, but that was no excuse for behaving like an animal, taking her standing up against a wall, for God's sake. When he had brought her here he had intended it to be like closing the circle. A new beginning. Instead he had only ended up hurting her even more.

Dios.

'Lily, I'm sorry.'

She didn't move. Only the barest nod of her head, rustling her hair against the pillow, showed that she had heard him. He sighed and raised himself up to sit on the edge of the bed, his back to her.

'I didn't mean for that to happen. I came after you to tell you that...' He paused, remembering with a cold, sickening feeling what she'd said. *I don't want love or tenderness or a happy ever after any more...* 'I just came to tell you that the answer is yes. I'll help you with the...the adoption.'

'You don't have to. I shouldn't have asked.' There was a note of resignation in her voice that turned him inside out.

He got up stiffly. 'No. You should. It's fine.' He looked down at her for a moment, feeling the knife in his gut twist. 'We'll work out some way of...being together.'

For a long moment their eyes held and a fathomless sea of unspoken words swelled between them.

'OK,' Lily said very quietly. 'Thank you.'

'It's the least I can do.'

He went over to the chair that stood against the wall and sat down.

'What are you doing?' she said in a small voice.

'I'll sleep here tonight.'

He hadn't expected her to argue, but it still hurt that she didn't. She lay down with a soft sigh and turned her back towards him, reminding him unbearably of the time in the hospital. In the soft grey light he watched her, until the delicate ridge of her spine, her creamy shoulder, the pale undersides of her narrow feet had faded into the gathering darkness.

CHAPTER FOURTEEN

'So, Mrs Romero... It's all right if I call you Mrs Romero, is it? Only I don't think your full name, or—er—your *title* would fit on the forms.'

'No, no, of course. That's fine.' Lily caught the sharp, critical edge in Miss Squires's voice, but forced herself to ignore it. She could call Lily whatever she damn well liked as long as it brought her closer to getting a child at the end of all this.

They were sitting in the Primrose Hill garden in the shade of the cherry tree. Laying the little French café table with a polka dotted cloth earlier Lily had hoped that Miss Squires would be won round by the rectangle of lawn that would be perfect for kicking a ball around, and the cherry tree that was crying out for a pram beneath it. But that was before she'd met Miss Squires. She looked as if it would take a lot more to win her round—a lifetime subscription to an ecological group and a fondness for knitting, for a start. Lily watched as she busily ticked boxes on the paper in front of her, trying not to let her heart sink.

'Please forgive me for asking,' said Miss Squires with a little laugh. 'We don't have a huge number of marquesas applying for adoption. Your husband would say the same about the title, would he—*if* he were here?'

'Absolutely. My husband never uses his title. It's really an irrelevance.'

Miss Squires's thin brows shot up beyond the rim of her

glasses and she quickly wrote something on the paper. 'So, where exactly is he, Mrs Romero? It is usual for us to see both partners at a home assessment meeting, you know.'

'I know,' Lily said quickly, 'and he sends his most sincere apologies. He got held up at work, but he'll be here any moment now.' Tristan had telephoned half an hour ago to say that he'd just landed the helicopter at London City Airport and was on his way. The bit about apologising sincerely was a slight over-statement.

'And where does he work?'

'Barcelona.'

'I see.' Miss Squires' tone suggested she'd been to Barcelona and not enjoyed the experience.

'In a bank,' Lily added desperately, as if that made it better somehow. She suppressed a sigh of sheer frustration and sprang to her feet. 'Let me just get some more biscuits,' she said, pick-ing up the empty plate and going towards the house. Anything to buy a few moments of breathing space. She had understood that the process would be difficult, but already she felt as if she were taking part in some kind of examination where the questions were in code.

The kitchen was quiet in the buttery late morning sunlight. A salmon she was marinading in the hope that it might make it look as if she and Tristan often shared cosy dinners at home lay on a dish on the side. As Lily arranged the last of the biscuits—home-made that morning; was that good or did it show she had too much time on her hands?—on the plate she had the feeling its glassy eye was looking at her critically.

Get a grip, she told herself shortly. After all, if she, with her commitment to the programme, couldn't cope, how the hell could she expect Tristan to?

Miss Squires looked up as she came back outside into the sunlight. 'I can see from my notes that you haven't been mar-ried very long, Mrs Romero. Just a year. That's a very short time compared to other couples on our waiting list. I think I remember reading about your marriage in the newspapers. It was rather sudden, wasn't it?'

Lily's heart plummeted as she set the biscuits down on the table. *Oh, God. Our adoption process is being handled by someone who reads the tabloids.* For a split second it crossed her mind that Miss Squires was not actually a local authority social worker but an undercover journalist out to get to the definitive story on the Romero marriage. The press interest in this subject had been intense over the past few weeks, and Tristan had an unfailing instinct for courting it to perfection, with the result that a rash of pictures had appeared in papers of them walking hand in hand on Primrose Hill, or kissing outside the house.

Seeing these pictures always cut Lily to the core.

Forcing her mind back to the question, she attempted what she hoped was a confident smile.

'Not really' she said, resisting the urge to cross her fingers. 'I'm afraid the papers don't always know the full story.'

Miss Squires looked a little piqued at this, and Lily realised she'd scored a hollow victory. 'I see. Would you say that press attention is a major issue for you and your husband?'

'Yes—I mean, no.' Lily felt the heat rise to her cheeks. There was no point in trying to hide the truth over this—the woman would have had to have been an illiterate Martian not to have been aware of the paparazzi interest in their marriage and Tristan's reputation as a reformed playboy, but she sensed it would not go down well to be too honest. 'Obviously we both have a reasonably high profile, so it's something we have to live with, but we're planning to move out of London in the near future, which will give us a lot more privacy.'

'I see. And where are you planning on moving to?'

'We've found a house in Cornwall, by the sea. It's deep in the countryside, miles from anywhere really, which should keep the paparazzi away.' Lily couldn't stop the smile from spreading across her face as she spoke. Dolphin House was perfect—closer to her childhood dream than she had ever dared to hope, with a yard at the back for chickens and a little sunny paddock where they could keep a pony. It also came with a mile of private beach. Miss Squires didn't have to know that what it didn't come with was Tristan, on any long-term basis anyway.

Lily dragged her mind away from the edge of that particularly lethal chasm, back to what the social worker was saying.

'...very isolated. We find our children thrive in communities where there is access to support groups and social workers and other families coping with similar issues. You might like to reconsider a move away from London at this stage. We recommend that change is kept to a minimum during the adoption process, since it inevitably disrupts things. For that reason we also insist that, whatever fertility problems you may have had, you resume using contraception. What method would be best for you?'

Lily couldn't stop a bitterly ironic laugh from escaping her. 'I can assure you there's no need for any method at all,' she said in a low voice. Tristan hadn't touched her since the night in the tower at Scarlet's wedding.

'Mrs Romero? Experience shows that even in couples who have experienced years of fertility difficulties, pregnancy can still occur, and for obvious reasons this would instantly eliminate you from the adoption procedure. Unless you're telling me that you and your husband have no sex life at all...'

She gave a little conspiratorial laugh at this, indicating that the idea of being in a sexless marriage with a man as gorgeous and famously sexy as Tristan Romero was utterly preposterous. Lily felt her nails digging into the palm of her hand.

She was right.

It was preposterous.

'I'm telling you that after I lost my baby the doctors had to operate to stop the bleeding,' Lily replied tonelessly. 'I had a hysterectomy. So you see, pregnancy would be a physical impossibility.'

'I see. And was Mr Romero supportive during that difficult time?'

Lily dropped her gaze to where her hands twisted the flower-sprigged cotton of her designed-to-look-wholesome skirt. From inside the house came a noise, like a door slamming.

'Yes,' Lily said quietly. Any minute now God was going to strike her down for all these lies, but in this case the truth wasn't really an option.

The older woman's face softened a little. 'What was it that first attracted you to him?'

Lily looked her straight in the eye. 'His strength. I don't mean physically, but he has this sort of aura about him that tells you you're safe. That he'll look after you, and somehow, no matter what, everything will be all right because he'll make it all right—'

'Why, thank you, *querida.*'

The dry, husky voice behind her made Lily jump. Whirling round in her seat, she saw Tristan standing in the kitchen door-way. He was dressed for the office, but his tie was loose and his collar unbuttoned and he held his jacket over one shoulder. For a moment their eyes met, and Lily felt the usual shyness that assaulted her afresh every time she saw him. Then, re-membering the presence of Miss Squires and its purpose, she got awkwardly to her feet.

Perhaps Tristan remembered at the same time, because as she went towards him he came down the steps to meet her, one arm outstretched to take her into an easy, loving embrace. He kissed her on the mouth, firmly, lingering just long enough to look like a husband who had been away and missed his wife.

Lily's heart turned over with gratitude.

And love, of course. But she was trying to wean herself off that particularly destructive habit.

'Darling, come and meet Miss Squires. She's going to be our case officer now we're starting the process properly. I'll make a fresh pot of tea.'

Tristan leaned over and took Miss Squires's rather limp

hand in his own strong one, and before she turned to go into the kitchen Lily saw the older woman colour slightly. As he sat down Miss Squires rearranged her papers busily and quite unnecessarily. 'So Mr Romero, I'm glad you could join us,' she said briskly. 'I've already had the chance to talk a bit to your wife, so now it's time to find out about you. Why don't you start by telling me about your parents?'

'What would you like to know?'

It was like being trapped in some private nightmare. An individually tailored version of his own personal hell, with every element hand-selected by sadists who knew his every weakness and wanted to expose his darkest fears.

And this particular sadist was disguised in a deceptively harmless-looking hand-knitted jumper and called herself a social worker. Tristan looked up at the leafy branches of the tree and made a conscious effort to relax, and not to show the tension that had suddenly turned his shoulders to granite. Lily's garden was lovely and usually he found the house in Primrose Hill oddly soothing after a high-pressure week in Barcelona or at one of the charitable projects, which he had now set up in two African countries as well as Khazakismir. Not today though. Right now even Tom's wedding reception seemed like a day at the seaside...

The voice of the social worker cut through his thoughts. She was looking at him steadily. 'What sort of childhood did you have?'

Tristan gave her a bland smile. 'Very privileged. I grew up in a big house with servants and a swimming pool. We were very lucky.'

'We? Who's we, Mr Romero? You and your brothers and sisters?'

Tristan felt the smile die on his lips, but kept it there with some effort. 'Me and my...brother.'

'Just one?'

Lily came out of the house carrying a tray. She was wearing

a simple white blouse with little cap sleeves and a short cotton skirt strewn with daisies that made her look fresh and pure and sweet. Tristan felt his heart lurch.

He had to do this for her.

'Yes,' he said, tersely. 'Just one. Nico. He's ten years younger than me. He works in a charity based in Madrid.'

Miss Squires was writing everything down, and Tristan was glad that her eyes were directed at the paper in front of her rather than at him.

'Not in the bank?'

'No.' Tristan had made sure of that. He'd sacrificed finishing his degree and doing something he wanted in life to make sure of that.

'What about your parents?' Miss Squires said, clearly deciding that Nico was of little interest. 'Are you close to them?'

Across the table Lily's eyes met his. They were soft and sunlight dappled, and they reached out to him. Looking into them, holding on, he said tonelessly, 'I see them quite often. I work alongside my father.'

Miss Squires looked up. 'That's not really what I'm asking.'

Gently Lily placed a pale blue pottery mug of tea in front of him. Tristan rubbed his fingers wearily across his eyes. 'Why do you want to know this?

'This is the next part of the process, Mr Romero,' said Miss Squires slightly archly. 'I think you've done the basic induction days, where you've heard a bit about some of the issues faced by the children in the adoption system?'

Tristan tried to keep the grimace from his face as he remembered the three grim Saturdays spent in a community centre in North London being told about the physical effects on babies born to mothers addicted to drugs or alcohol, the mental effects of neglect, violence or abuse.

Areas he was pretty much expert in already. At times he had felt like getting up and giving the talk himself.

'Well,' the social worker continued, with a small shake of

her head at Lily's offer of sugar, 'this is the time when we find out more about you. About what kind of person you are, which will help us match you to a child. We feel that the experiences people had when they were children play a crucial role in defining what kind of parents they'll end up becoming.'

No kidding.

'It's important to be as honest as you can—things have a habit of coming out further down the line anyway. Were you close to your mother, would you say?'

This must be how it feels to stand on the gallows, thought Tristan bleakly. *This realisation that there's no longer any possibility of running or hiding.* 'Not really,' he said stiffly. 'My mother's only close relationship is with alcohol, and I was sent to boarding school in England when I was eight.'

Behind her glasses the social worker blinked. 'How did you feel about that?'

'Absolutely delighted.'

Miss Squires looked deeply shocked, as if he'd just admitted to a fondness for torturing kittens. 'Really? So you're in favour of sending children away to be educated in impersonal institutions, away from the family?'

He met her eyes steadily. 'Yes, if the family is like mine was.'

Beneath the table Lily found his hand and took it in hers. The sunlight filtering through the cherry tree made her hair shimmer and turned her skin to honeyed gold. For a moment there was no sound apart from birdsong and the distant drone of an aeroplane in the cornflower-blue sky above.

'Could you explain that a bit more?'

Dios, was she never going to give up? Panic was beginning to close in on him, like a cloth coming down over his face, making it difficult to breathe, difficult to think. The tranquil garden with the cherry tree and the sound of birds seemed suddenly unreal, insubstantial and all he could see was the darkness inside himself.

Lily's hand was the only thing anchoring him to reality.

He felt her fingers tighten around his as the darkness sucked him down.

He laughed, and even to his own ears it was a horrible, harsh sound. 'My father is the eleventh Duke of Tarraco, and a direct descendent of one of the first *familiares*—collaborators of the Spanish Inquisition. That should tell you something. My family rose to prominence and gained wealth and favour from the royal court thanks to their fondness for the rack and the thumbscrew. Cruelty is a family trait.'

'Are you saying that your father was *cruel* to you, Mr Romero?' Miss Squires persisted.

'Of course not,' Tristan replied with deep, drawling irony. 'It wasn't *cruelty*. No—every blow, every lash of the belt, every stroke of the whip was for our own good. He wasn't being cruel to us, he was simply doing his *duty*, forging us into proper Romero men, making sure he passed on the legacy of violence and brutality to us, just as his father had passed it on to him.'

Lily's hand. Holding his. Keeping him from the edge. A part of his mind stayed fixed on that while he continued, almost conversationally, 'The Banco Romero was initially founded to process the money confiscated from victims of the Inquisition. In fact,' he drawled coldly, 'my family now own a set of priceless jewels that once belonged to someone that one of our distinguished ancestors had executed for heresy.'

Lily's face was pale, stricken, reflecting all the suffering he had taught himself not to show.

'The Romero jewels,' she whispered.

Tristan's smile was glacial. 'Exactly. A symbol of our corruption and guilt.'

'That's why you didn't want me to have them?'

Adrenaline was coursing through him and the chasm gaped before him, dark and deep and full of horror. He had to stay strong to stop himself slipping down into it. Pulling his hand from hers he shrugged. 'Yes. And because I can't look at them without remembering the night when my father ripped the earrings out of my mother's ears for some comment that she'd made over dinner that he considered disrespectful. So you see, it wasn't only me and my brothers who bore the brunt of it...'

His throat constricted suddenly, cutting off the terrible litany of memories, and Tristan brought his fist up to his forehead in a jerky, helpless movement. Lily had shifted forwards to the edge of her seat so that she was facing him, both her hands folded around his.

'Brothers?' Miss Squires enquired. Tristan felt his blood turn to ice as she glanced down at the paper she'd been writing on. 'I thought you only had one?'

He had to hand it to her, Tristan thought dully, dropping his head into his hands for a moment. She'd said that the truth had a habit of coming out. He lifted his head and looked straight at the social worker with a bitter smile.

'I do now. But once there were three of us. My older brother, Emilio was the true Romero heir. It should have been he who inherited the title and the position in the company.'

'What happened to him?' Lily asked in a whisper.

'He killed himself the day before his twenty-first birthday.'

CHAPTER FIFTEEN

'HE COULDN'T take it any more, you see. The pressure of being the Romero heir and the position in the bank, so he—'

Tristan's voice sounded as if he had swallowed broken glass. Numb with horror, Lily stumbled to her feet so that her chair fell backwards. 'Tristan, stop!' she said in a low wail of anguish, going to stand behind him and sliding her arms around his shoulders, trying to hold all of him. 'Please, stop now...you don't have to say any more.'

Across the table Miss Squires averted her eyes and wrote more notes.

In her arms Tristan's body felt utterly rigid, utterly unyielding, as if she were holding a block of stone. And then very slowly he unpeeled her arms from around him and got stiffly to his feet. Standing behind him, Lily couldn't see his face, but his voice was like black ice.

'Sorry.'

The tense little silence that followed was broken by the ring of a mobile phone, which made them all start. Tristan stooped to take it from the pocket of his jacket that hung on the back of the chair. 'Sorry,' he said again, but this time all trace of emotion had left his voice and the word was perfectly bland. 'I have to take this.' Slipping out from the table, he walked away into the house.

Miss Squires was gathering together her sheets of paper and tucking them into a folder. 'Well, I think we'll leave it there for today,' she said, tucking the folder back in her recycled hessian bag and carefully not meeting Lily's eye. For a moment Lily almost hated her for making Tristan talk about those things. But she hated herself more. She had made him do this.

They got up and went through the kitchen and into the hallway. It was cool in here, and, after the sunlit garden, very dim. Tristan's voice drifted down the stairs, strong, staccato, decisive. At the door Miss Squires turned to Lily with a rather forced smile. 'Thank you for the tea, Mrs Romero, and I'll be in touch about our next meeting.' She paused. 'If you and your husband decide to proceed, that is.'

Outside Lily gathered up the mugs and the plate of biscuits she had laid out with such high hopes and such meticulous care. How foolish it seemed now that she had thought that biscuits and the kind of skirt she wore were important when all the time she hadn't known anything about what really mattered. She carried the tray into the kitchen and set it down beside the salmon. The carefully chosen, stage managed salmon that had played its part to perfection, and which Miss Squires hadn't even seemed to notice. She looked up as Tristan appeared in the doorway.

'I have to go.'

She froze, and the apology she had been about to deliver died on her lips. There was something terrifyingly bleak about the way he spoke. Something final that invited no further discussion. His face had a waxen quality about it and his lips were white.

'Tristan, what is it? What's happened?'

He shook his head quickly, backing away from her with his hands held in front of him, as if he wanted to hold her off him.

'An emergency. Dimitri is waiting outside. I'm sorry, I have to leave immediately.' He turned, running a hand through his hair distractedly as he looked around before moving into the hallway. 'It's probably for the best, anyway.'

'What do you mean?'

He shrugged, terrifying in his bleakness. 'I've ruined it for you.'

'No,' Lily said fiercely. 'I should never have asked you to do this. It was stupid and selfish.' She bit her lip, struggling to keep the anguish and the pain from her voice. 'You even tried to say no, and then I made you change your mind.'

He gave a harsh laugh. One hand was on the open door, the knuckles gleaming like pearls. 'After...the baby, how could I not? How could I not help?'

Duty. That was what had made him do this for her.

Of course.

She remembered the look on his face just after they'd made love, just before he'd agreed to do it. The look of a man who was enduring torment.

People said that when you were stabbed you didn't feel the pain at first. That there was a strange numb sensation of tingling heat before the pain kicked in. Lily knew that she had to speak while she still could. Before the pain started and she couldn't do anything. On the street beyond the gate his long black car crouched menacingly, Dimitri's expressionless face just visible through the glass. Fixing her eyes on it, Lily said hoarsely, 'You'd better go.'

'Yes.'

He hesitated, head bent, looking as if there was something else he wanted to say. Lily waited, her breath burning in her chest, her torn heart still as he lifted his head and gave her a twisted, heartbreaking smile.

'I'm sorry,' he said, and walked away.

He didn't look back, didn't turn his head as the car pulled away. Because if he had he might have told Dimitri to stop and he would have got out and gone back to her. He imagined running back up the path towards her and snatching her up in his arms and kissing her hard enough to tell her what he didn't have the words to say.

No, it wasn't that he didn't have the words. He knew exactly what words he wanted to say, but the Romero curse of duty and honour made it impossible to say them because he knew that telling Lily Alexander that he loved her would be a singularly selfish act. What could he offer her? Tainted wealth and a heart so damaged and twisted it was barely recognisable as human. Nothing that she wanted or needed. He thought of what Tom had said all those months ago at Stowell, about her needing someone nice and steady. Someone who could help her fulfil her dream of becoming a mother, not stand in the way of it.

Feeling infinitely weary, he kept his eyes fixed straight ahead until they had left the narrow network of streets around Lily's house, the restaurant where he'd once kissed her for the benefit of a photographer he'd spotted lurking in a car parked further up the street, the stretch of open ground on Primrose Hill where they'd walked sometimes, holding hands. He smiled ruefully to himself. In these last few months he'd really learned to love the paparazzi.

When they reached the wide, impersonal road around Regent's Park he turned to Dimitri, making a huge effort to turn outwards from his own tragedy to the wider suffering.

'So how bad is it?'

Behind his glasses Dimitri's face was grey. 'Earthquake was six point eight on Richter Scale. Epicentre about thirty kilometers to the north of the village.'

Tristan's mind raced. Below seven on the Richter scale. That was encouraging. He turned his head and gazed unseeingly out of the window where it was business as usual in London. People were going about life oblivious to the disaster on the other side of the world, the smaller one a few miles away in Primrose Hill.

'The health centre?'

'Some damage, but still standing.'

He nodded, briefly. Khazakismir lay a little to the north of the East Anatolian fault, and Tristan had ensured that the health centre was built to the latest earthquake construction standards. Unlike most of the other buildings in the village.

'Irina?'

'I do not know…' Dimitri's voice cracked. 'The house is gone. They have not found her yet. Or the twins. We just have to hope.'

'Yes. There's always hope,' lied Tristan.

The bright morning had faded into a dull afternoon and a wind had sprung up. It whipped the polka-dotted cloth off the table in the garden and hurled it across the lawn.

Lily was cold. So cold that she couldn't remember what it had felt like to be warm. In the hours since Tristan had left she had been pacing around the house, numbly going about the business of sorting, ordering, tidying away, almost as if she were getting ready to leave. Going upstairs to get a jumper, she saw the ivory satin dress that Tristan had bought her hanging in the wardrobe, and she finally gave way to tears.

It was over. The last infinitely fine silken thread that had tied her to Tristan had been severed and he had gone, leaving her in the ruins of a life with which she felt no connection. All the things she'd wanted, all the dreams she had spent so many years building in her head had crumbled into ashes and dust the moment she had tried to grasp hold of them.

As the clouds gathered and blackened outside she moved through the house like a sleepwalker, shivering, picking things up and putting them back in different places, tears falling erratically and unheeded as she tidied up the loose ends from which she had hoped to make a life. She found the estate agent's brochure on Dolphin House, with its glossy photographs of the huge sun-filled kitchen, the master bedroom, the view from the beautiful landing window over the garden to the sea, and remembered how she had imagined living there, with the children she was going to make hers. She had told Miss Squires over the phone that she would be open to taking any child, no matter what its background or problems, because she had believed there was no damage that couldn't be overcome with love.

But she had been wrong.

She had loved Tristan, and she hadn't been able to reach him at all. She had never managed to break through the shell of duty and obligation and touch the damaged heart beneath. Instead she had just become another one of the people for whom he felt responsible.

Duty, not love. That was what had bound him to her. He had told her that he was incapable of love, incapable of any emotion, but on some level she had thought she could change that.

Fix him.

She wiped her sleeve impatiently across one wet cheek. How was it possible to be so arrogant and at the same time so naïve? She hadn't even tried to find out what had made him like that in the first place—into the kind of man who didn't show a flicker of emotion when his own child died.

In the kitchen the salmon fixed her with its baleful, accusing eye. *What difference would it have made if you knew?* it seemed to say. *He just didn't love you and he didn't want the baby. Nothing could have changed that.*

'Shut up,' she said out loud, and, opening the back door in a gust of wind, she picked it up and put it outside for the little grey cat.

The house seemed terrifyingly quiet. Pulling the sleeves of her jumper down over her hands, she wandered through to the sitting room and switched on the television, finally stopping her pacing and sinking down into the embrace of the old velvet sofa and drawing her knees up to her chest. The screen in front of her was filled with the images of some distant disaster, of people sifting through the rubble of what had been houses with bare hands, grey with dust. The noise, condensed and filtered through the speakers of the television, was that of collective pain, and Lily recognised that the people she was watching were engaged in what she, in her own way, had spent the time doing since Tristan left. Trying to make order out of chaos. Hoping for some sign that it was worth carrying on.

An earthquake, read the rolling titles at the bottom of the screen. In the remote northern territories of Khazakismir.

Hundreds feared dead. The authoritative voice of the news-reader painted colour into the bare details of lunchtime in the middle of an ordinary day when an act of God had brought destruction of a more thorough and impersonal kind to people used to bombs and machine guns. An aid organisation already had an established base in the region, he said, and was working on the ground, doing what it could until an international effort could be launched.

Numbly Lily watched, her own grief not diminished by the suffering she saw in front of her, but somehow put into context by larger sorrow. Life was painful. All you could do was find someone to hold onto.

And hope that you didn't lose them.

When the mobile phone rang beside her she leapt up and seized it immediately, irrationally hoping that it might be Tristan, but the voice on the other end of the line was female. Disappointment hit her like a blow to the stomach, doubling her up as she sank back onto the sofa again, barely focusing on what the woman on the other end of the line was saying. Distractedly she turned the television to mute.

'Señor Romero?'

'No, I'm sorry. He's not here.'

'But that is his phone, is it not? I am trying to contact him on a matter of urgency.'

With a thud of surprise Lily realised that the phone in her hand was Tristan's, and that he must have accidentally put it down after he took the call earlier.

'Yes, this is his phone, but I'm afraid he left—' she looked at the clock above the fireplace '—maybe five or six hours ago.' Was that all? It felt like days ago that they had sat in the garden in the sunshine with the social worker. 'I don't expect him to come back,' Lily added bleakly.

'Do you know where he was going?'

She was Spanish, Lily registered. She sounded young and self-possessed and sexy. Not like the kind of person to spend an afternoon huddled on a sofa in the half-darkness, mesmerised by misery.

'He left because there was some crisis at work. You could try him at the bank,' she said without thinking, and then regretted it. Why was she helping this woman to get in touch with *her* husband?

'No,' said the voice impatiently. 'I am calling from the bank. I am Bianca, his secretary. He is not here, and there was no crisis at work until a moment ago. Señora, I need to find him urgently. It is his father—he has had a heart attack and is in hospital. Señora? Are you still there?'

Lily heard her.

She heard, but at that moment she was unable to respond. Letting the phone slide down until she was clutching it to her chest, she stood up in the sad early evening darkness and stared, dumbstruck, at the bright screen in front of her.

A news reporter stood amid the devastation of what was once a village, his face grave, his mouth opening and closing as he spoke to camera, while behind him workers moved rubble with their bare hands.

Tristan.

One of them was Tristan.

CHAPTER SIXTEEN

LILY's first thought was that it was someone else. Someone tall and dark, with the same high cheekbones and square jaw, but as she watched he straightened up, raising his arm and issuing directions, sweeping his hand across his face as he glanced into the camera for a moment.

And then he turned away, and the camera cut back to the London studio and Lily realised she had walked over to the television and sunk down to her knees in front of the screen.

She blinked, her eyes stinging, and suddenly remembered that she was still holding the phone.

'Bianca? Sorry, I'm still here. What did you say?'

'His father is very ill, señora. They do not know at this stage whether he will survive. I need to inform Señor Romero, but I don't know where to find him.'

'It's all right,' Lily said faintly. 'I do.' She paused. 'Bianca—I don't suppose... I mean, would you possibly know how to go about organising some kind of private flight?'

'Of course.' Bianca sounded slightly condescending. 'I do it all the time.'

'Good. Then get me a flight from London to Khazakismir. I want to leave tonight.'

Too late Tristan spotted the film crew.

He had arrived in the village a little over an hour ago, having spent the flight with the satellite phone continuously jammed up against his ear as he organised for manpower to be deflected from projects in other parts of the world and flown out to Khazakismir, along with medical teams and the first wave of supplies. The most important thing in the immediate aftermath of a disaster was organisation, and Tristan's utter lack of faith in the Khazakismiri government and army meant it was vital that someone was there to make sure the immediate relief effort was co-ordinated and efficient.

That was what he had been thinking of as he stood in the centre of the village. That, and the fact that Dimitri had just been told by a neighbour of Irina's that his sister's lifeless body had been pulled from the chaos that used to be her kitchen a few hours ago. He hadn't been thinking of the journalists that had miraculously managed to appear on the scene when Nico and countless other of his aid workers were still battling through red tape to get there. But as soon as he looked up into the dark eye of the camera he knew he had slipped up.

Turning away, he wiped the dust from his face and looked around for Dimitri. He knew, in some distant part of his brain, that in the sophisticated game of bluff and counter bluff that he had been playing with the newspapers and the paparazzi for years he had just made a very grave tactical error. One that could just spell his defeat.

The thing was he didn't care.

Lily barely had time to pack a few things into a bag before Bianca rang back. A plane was ready to leave immediately from London City Airport, she said. Lily was about to protest that it would take her some time to get there when from down below she heard the sound of the doorbell. *'Bueno,'* Bianca said crisply from Barcelona. 'There is your car. I have arranged for someone to meet you at the airport in Khazakismir. Have a good flight, and please ask Señor Romero to contact me as soon as possible.'

So this was Tristan's world, thought Lily numbly as the small, luxurious Citation jet launched itself upwards into the dark night. A world where you could go wherever you wanted to go at a moment's notice, where there were rafts of people to make the arrangements for you and pick you up and drop you off. But no one for you to talk to. No one you could confide in.

Below her London lay in a glittering sprawl, and Lily felt as if a band were tightening around her chest as the lights grew smaller and fainter in the spreading pool of blackness. She was leaving behind everything that was familiar and hurtling out into the unknown. She hadn't really had time to think about what she was doing and had acted purely on instinct. Looking down, she noticed with a thud of dismay that she was still wearing the flower-sprigged skirt and thin shirt that seemed to belong to another lifetime.

The smiling steward appeared beside her and reeled off a long list of the drinks and snacks on offer, as if Lily were flying off on some indulgent holiday. It had been a long time since the tea and biscuits with Miss Squires, and she wasn't sure when she would get the chance to eat again, so she asked for coffee and a club sandwich that she really didn't want and picked up the evening paper that had been left on the table.

The front page was dominated by pictures of the earthquake. Buildings leant at drunken angles next to those that had completely collapsed, leaving only wires and steel joists sticking up into the dusty air like fractured bones. Lily's sandwich went untouched as her eyes skimmed the columns of print.

Tristan's name leapt out at her, almost as if it had been printed in foot high letters and highlighted in neon rather than mentioned in a narrow sidebar under a small heading. 'Playboy shows his serious side. Full story pages 6-7.'

Lily's hands were shaking so much she could hardly turn the pages.

It was a double page spread. The headline that stretched across both pages was THE PARTY'S OVER FOR EUROPE'S BAD-BOY BILLIONAIRE and beneath it was a row of photographs showing Tristan with his arm around a variety of beauties at parties and in nightclubs. 'Never the same girl twice!' said the caption underneath. The photo in the centre was bigger, and showed him sitting alone in the back of a car.

Lily's heart stopped.

The picture had clearly been taken with a long-lens camera through a blacked out window. Tristan's head was tipped back against the headrest, his eyes were closed, but the flash of the camera had clearly picked up the tears glistening on his cheeks. The caption beneath read: *'Suffering: A clearly devastated Tristan Romero de Losada Montalvo leaves the hospital where his wife was taken after miscarrying their child earlier this year.'*

The smiling steward appeared at her side. 'Is there anything you'd like, Mrs Romero?'

Oh, God, thought Lily. Where to start to answer that question?

How about *my husband's forgiveness*?

Tristan sat on a hard wooden pew in the village church, his head tipped back against the wall.

His eyes were closed but he wasn't asleep. He wouldn't let himself sleep because, although every muscle and every cell in his body screamed with exhaustion, he knew he had to stay awake and keep holding onto the baby in his arms. Behind his closed eyelids the events of the night before replayed themselves in a constant, tightening loop, so that repeatedly he relived the moment when he had heard the baby crying, then the frantic, adrenaline-fuelled desperation to try to reach it and the feeling of suffocation when he'd finally crawled into the tiny gap between the collapsed roof joist and the rubble of bricks and plaster that had once been the walls to Irina's house.

And that was the part where the film kept stalling, like a tape getting stuck and then jerking backwards. He could see the baby—see her small foot in its dirty pink sleepsuit, kicking and flexing, but as he reached out his hand, ramming his shoulder into the narrow space between the roof beam and a slab of wall, it seemed always to slip through his fingers...

He came to with a cry, his arms tightening reflexively around the bundle in his arms, his eyes flying open and widening in horror as he looked down at the empty blanket clutched to his chest...

'It's OK. Tristan, it's all right. She's safe, look—she's here.'

Lily.

It was Lily, standing over him and cradling the sleeping baby in her arms.

Tristan dropped his head into his hands, rubbing his fingers hard into eyes that still felt as if they were full of grit. He wasn't sure any more if he was asleep or awake. Was this just another scene in his disjointed series of dreams?

He heard the quiet whisper of her skirt as she sat down beside him. The skirt she had been wearing in the garden when the social worker came, he thought randomly; was it a day or a month or a lifetime ago? And then he caught a breath of her clean milk and almonds fragrance and he knew that she was really there.

Slowly he lifted his head and straightened up, feeling his muscles protest at every movement. Lily said nothing, but she took his hand in her free one, and they just sat like that for a while, his rough, grit-encrusted fingers entwined with her cool, pale, clean ones, her head leaning very lightly against his shoulder, listening to the sound of the baby's breathing.

'Why did you come?' he said at last. His voice was rusty and his throat ached from shouting last night. Shouting instructions to Nico, and Dimitri and hundreds of others who were engaged in the same race against time to free those trapped in the rubble.

She sighed softly and shifted just a little on the pew, so that she was facing him more, her grey eyes serious. 'Bianca called. Your father had a heart attack yesterday. A serious one. They don't think he'll survive.'

Tristan exhaled heavily, tipping his head back again as despair came down like the night. Not for Juan Carlos, but because he had thought, for a moment, that Lily had come because she wanted him. Because she loved him.

'You came all the way here to tell me that?'

'I thought you might want to see him, before he died,' she said quietly. She was rocking the baby very gently, almost imperceptibly, in an instinctive maternal rhythm as old as time. 'I wanted you to have that chance, before it's too late.'

'I'm afraid it's been a wasted journey,' he snapped. 'Juan Carlos can go to the corner of hell he reserved for himself years ago without any kind of goodbye from me.' He looked up, frowning as a thought suddenly struck him. 'How did you know where to find me?'

'Oh, you know, the usual way wives know where their husbands are,' she said with gentle irony. 'There was a report about the earthquake on the news and I saw you in the background.'

He gave a ragged laugh. 'That's it, then. Game over. The press will no doubt pick it up and then—'

'They're onto it already. Does it matter?'

'Yes,' he said very wearily. 'I don't know; probably.'

She had been looking down at the child in her arms, but now she lifted her head and looked at him, and the intensity in her beautiful eyes made his sore throat close. 'Why?' she said fiercely. 'Because now everyone will know that Tristan Romero has a heart? That behind the cold façade of the womanising billionaire businessman there's actually a man who cares about people?'

He leaned back in the hard pew, trying to ease the ache in his back and his arms and his shoulders and his heart. 'Is there?' he said cynically. 'Or is that just a new image, a fresh angle that they'll use to sell papers?'

'I think you care,' she said huskily.

'OK,' he admitted, on a heavy outward breath, 'I care. *Dios*, Lily, I *care* so much…but what's the point when I can't help the people I care about? I let you down yesterday, by saying too much. I ruined it for you. My toxic past just keeps coming back to poison your life, doesn't it?'

She got to her feet while he was speaking and stood in front of him, shifting the baby easily up onto her shoulder, cupping the downy hair that was still matted with grit and dust in her hand. Her face was creased with anguish. 'Tristan, that doesn't matter,' she said and her voice was low and urgent. 'None of that matters. I should never, never have put you through that, but at least it made me realise that the most important thing—'

Just then the door at the back of the church burst open and the tranquillity was momentarily disturbed by the sound of heavy feet hurrying across the tiled floor. People sitting quietly in the pews praying or huddled in little groups giving comfort to each other looked round.

'Señor Romero!'

Quickly Lily slipped out of the pew and went towards Dimitri, taking his hand. His face was wet with tears.

'Dimitri, what is it?'

'Oh, Marquesa,' he sobbed, 'they have found Andrei!'

Tristan had got to his feet and was standing perfectly still, his face white and tense beneath the streaks of dirt. Agony shot through Lily as an image of him standing by the window in the hospital suddenly flashed into her head, and she recognised the same desperate attempt to maintain emotional control. How could she have been stupid enough to think he didn't care?

'Is he alive?' Tristan said tersely.

'Yes. Dehydrated. He is on drip in health centre, but he will be all right soon.' Dimitri's expression of tentative joy wavered again as he glanced at the baby against Lily's chest. 'How is Emilia?

'She's fine,' Lily soothed. 'Sleeping peacefully. She's so beautiful, Dimitri.'

Dimitri looked down at the floor and shuffled his feet in helpless misery. 'Yes. Just like Irina when she was small.' His voice broke. 'They have no one now.'

'Dimitri, they have you,' Lily said softly, and she held out the sleeping baby to him. Clumsily he took her into his arms and held her awkwardly, but his hands just seemed too big to manage the fragile bundle and the expression on his fleshy, implacable face was one of pained bewilderment.

'I cannot care for them,' he said hopelessly. 'Khazakismiri men not brought up to look after babies. I not know how to start now, after so many years without a wife and family. If I was younger perhaps…' He thrust the baby back to Lily almost imploringly. 'But you could care for them, Marquesa. You and Señor Romero—'

'It's out of the question.'

Tristan leapt to his feet and he pushed past Lily, walking a little distance away before swinging round to face them both. Beneath the grime his face was pale and taut with fury. 'There are legal procedures. It's not simple.'

'Sorry, Señor.' Dimitri looked stricken. 'Sorry. I should not have asked. It is a miracle that they are safe, but now I worry about what will happen to them…'

Lily laid a hand on Dimitri's arm. 'It's perfectly natural that you're worried, but try not to think about that now. It's too early to make any plans for the twins' future yet, but of course I'll take care of them for the time being, for as long as it takes to sort something out.' Dimitri's face broke into a relieved smile. 'On one condition,' she added.

'Marquesa…?'

'That you go and get something to eat and some rest.'

After Dimitri had gone, Lily carefully laid Emilia down in the makeshift bed someone had provided for her and went to where Tristan was standing, leaning with his back against a wall by the altar, his eyes closed. The old stone church had withstood the earthquake, but the stained glass window above his head was broken, and coloured shards of glass crunched beneath Lily's feet as she went towards him. Her heart was hammering, a sickening drumbeat of quiet dread.

'It seems so obvious, doesn't it?' he said bitterly, without opening his eyes. 'And I know that it's what you want more than anything, but I can't do it, Lily.'

She was aware of pain crouching in the corners of her mind, inching forwards, waiting to strike when he said the words that would spell the end, once and for all. She stopped a few feet away from him, clasping her hands together and pressing them to her lips.

'No. It's OK. I understand.'

Still his eyes stayed shut, his long lashes dark against his white cheeks. His brow was creased as if he was in pain. 'Do you?'

'Yes.' It was barely more than a whisper. 'You never wanted to get married. You never wanted children. You said all along you'd never love me. So, yes, I understand why you can't do it.'

His eyes flew open and he pushed himself violently away from the wall, taking her by the shoulders and staring down into her face with an expression of intense suffering that tore into her, filling her with anguish but also a peculiar kind of hope.

'No! I love you more than I thought it was possible to love anyone…anything.' He spoke slowly, clearly, his voice raw with terrible emotion. 'God, Lily—I love you so much it's killing me, because I can't give you the one thing that you want and because loving you means that I *have* to do what's best for you, and that's leave you alone.'

She shook her head, vehemently in denial. *'No—'*

'Yes.' Still holding her by the shoulders, he shook her slightly, his eyes searing into hers. 'Because I can't risk it. What if I turn out to be like him?'

'Your father?

'Yes. Him and all the other Romero men before him.' He let her go abruptly, stepping back and raising his clenched fists to his temples. 'You were right when you said I was afraid, though it took me a long time to admit it to myself. But I'm absolutely bloody terrified, Lily. I'm scared witless that somewhere that behaviour has been branded into me, hardwired into my brain, and that whether I mean to or not I'll just end up repeating the cycle.'

Hope flickered, a tiny flame in the darkness. She smiled steadily into the deep blue anguish of his eyes. 'You won't.'

'You don't know that,' he said fiercely. 'Look at you—you're a natural. It's who you are. You look after things—from injured birds to stray cats. It's instinctive. Intuitive. Whereas I'm—'

'Like that too.'

'No!' He took an angry step forward, thrusting his hands into his pockets, almost as if he was afraid he might hurt her. 'My instinct is to run away from anything remotely emotional,' he said in a voice that dripped with self-disgust. 'I'm the man who tried to buy you off, remember? I'm the man who tried to pay to have nothing to do with my own child. I'm the man who left you on your own when you were pregnant, and wasn't there when—'

Lily didn't move, didn't flinch. 'No,' she said quietly. 'You're not that man. That wasn't instinct. That was desperation. Your instinct was to be the man who holds a little girl's hand in church when she drops her flowers. Your instinct was to put your younger brother before yourself. That was why you dropped out of university, wasn't it?'

He nodded, almost imperceptibly, his eyes fixed on hers. Lily didn't miss a beat, continuing in the same gentle, hypnotic voice. 'Your instinct was to look after a pregnant woman on the other side of the world, and provide for whole communities and bring hope to people whose lives have been torn apart. Your instinct was to risk your own life to rescue a child. Tristan, I watched you when you were asleep…' for the first time her voice caught, and she moved towards him '…and you were holding the blanket as if you were still cradling her in your arms. Even then, even when you were half dead with exhaustion, your instinct was to protect her.'

'Do you think so?'

The expression on his face was one of exquisite torment, and it took all Lily's powers of self restraint not to throw herself into his arms and kiss away the hurt. But she couldn't do that. Not yet. She stood a few inches away from him trembling with longing and hope.

'I *know* so. I *know* that as well as being the man I want to be married to for the rest of my life, you'd also make the most fantastic, incredible father.' She took a deep breath as her eyes blurred with hot, stinging tears. 'But that doesn't mean that we have to do this, Tristan. You were wrong when you said that this is the one thing I want. It's not. I'd be lying if I said I didn't still want children, but only with you. Only if we're doing it together, and if it's not what you want then just having you will be enough for me because...'

Here she faltered, and bowed her head as the tears ran down her face and splashed on the dusty floor. For a moment neither of them moved, and then she felt Tristan very gently take her chin between his fingers and lift her face to his. His blue eyes burned with passion and pain.

'Because what?' he said hoarsely.

'Because I love you so much.'

He scowled down at her, trying to take it in. 'So much that you'd give up your dream for me?'

'You are my dream,' she said simply. 'It all begins and ends with you. And if some day, somehow, we had a family then that would be...amazing, but if we didn't, then I'd still have more than I had any right to wish for.' She paused, her eyelids flickering closed for a second, almost as if she were praying. '*If* I had you.'

Tristan gave a moan of helpless longing. 'You have me. Oh, *Dios*, Lily, you have me, for all of eternity...'

As he bent his head to kiss her Lily saw a tear fall, leaving a clean trail through the grime on his cheek, and as his lips met hers she felt them tremble. He kissed her with slow and tender passion that felt almost like reverence, his hands cupping her face, his heart beating against hers. And then when both of them were gasping for breath and his fingers were wet with her tears he folded her into his body and wrapped his arms tightly around her, and just held her.

After a long time Lily raised her head and looked up at him.

'Is it wrong to be happy in the midst of all this devastation?' she whispered.

Tristan shook his head slowly. 'No. It's the only thing that's right. The only thing that makes sense. The only thing that makes it possible to go on from this. And we will, I promise you we will.'

Strength and certainty blazed in the depths of the blue eyes Lily loved so much. She closed her eyes and leaned her head against him.

'Tristan, please...' she said quietly, 'hold me again. Don't let go.'

'I won't,' he whispered fiercely into her hair. 'I'll never let go.

EPILOGUE

LILY paused, a little blue birthday candle held between her fingers as she stood at the window of the big sunny kitchen.

Outside the garden swooned in the syrupy heat of the summer afternoon and the sea sparkled in the distance. At the far side of the lawn a table stood, half in the shade of the huge cedar tree whose branches were hung with brightly striped bunting, and Emilia's squeals of delighted laughter drifted across the drowsy air and in through the open door.

Lily's face broke into a smile of pure adoration as she watched her, delicious in the pink tutu and fairy wings Scarlet and Tom had given her, sitting on the bit of Scarlet's knee that wasn't taken up with the bulk of advanced pregnancy and giggling infectiously as Scarlet tickled her plump little arms with the feather-trimmed fairy wand.

At the other end of the table Andrei sat in his highchair carefully scrutinising the wooden fire engine that Dimitri had given him. Lily's heart clenched with helpless love. He was quieter, more timid and reserved than his easy-going sister, his small face was solemn, setting him slightly apart from the celebration going on around him.

It was a double celebration: for the twins' first birthday and also to toast their permanent acceptance into Lily and Tristan's lives. The interim care order that had allowed them to bring them home to Cornwall had at last been approved as a formal adoption, in no small part thanks to the efforts of Miss Squires who had turned out to be a staunch ally. Her report had stated that Tristan's own difficult past, and the strength and courage with which he had dealt with it, made him ideally placed to care for the twins.

Tristan joked that she had supported them solely so that she had an excuse to keep coming down to Dolphin House and seeing Dimitri, who sat beside her now with his arm thrown protectively round the back of her chair, his careworn face serene. Next to him Nico leaned back in his chair and laughed at something Tom had said, and his laid-back, charismatic charm reminded Lily with sudden piercing poignancy of the beautiful stranger who had jumped down from the helicopter and pulled her straight into his arms a lifetime ago.

She gasped as those same strong arms slid around her from behind, and the same lips that had flamed ecstasy into her body and changed her life for ever brushed the nape of her neck. Their touch was gentle and loving now, but still powerful enough to make the earth tilt on its axis.

'All right *cariño mio*?' Tristan murmured against her skin, his warm breath sending shivers of delicate joy down her spine.

'Mmm...' she sighed, closing her eyes. 'Although if you carry on like that I might just have to keep everyone waiting for the cake.'

Tristan pulled her close, wrapping his arms around her. 'That would be a shame.' His mouth was close to her ear and she could hear the smile in his voice. 'It is, after all, the most fantastic cake ever.'

Together they looked at the fairy tale castle Lily had painstakingly constructed from sponge and chocolate buttercream, and she smiled as she placed the pink candle alongside the blue one in the top of the turret, next to the tiny sugar-icing dove. Then, kissing the side of her neck, Tristan let her go and went to the fridge to take out a bottle of champagne. Sucking chocolate buttercream from her fingers, Lily dreamily watched him open the bottle.

'Shouldn't you wait and open that outside?'

Suddenly serious, Tristan shook his head as he poured pale golden fizz into two glasses. 'Today is for Andrei and Emilia, but this is a private toast to us.' He handed one to her. 'To *you*— for loving me when I didn't deserve to be loved and giving me more than I ever dared to hope for.' He kissed her lingeringly on the mouth and glanced out of the window to the table beneath the tree. 'Today feels a bit like the wedding we never had.'

Lovingly, Lily's fingers traced the outline of his lips, the indentation in his chin. 'We never had the wedding,' she murmured, kissing the corner of his mouth, 'but we have the marriage, which is what matters.'

She felt his lips curve into a rueful, sexy smile. 'Come on. If we stay in here much longer I won't be responsible for my actions, and if Miss Squires finds me making love to you on the kitchen floor she might just change her mind about my suitability as a parent.'

He picked up the open bottle and took another one from the fridge while Lily lit the candles on the cake. Holding aloft her fragile cargo, Lily followed her husband out into the sunlit garden.

The air was scented with summer and the sea. As they crossed the lawn Tom saw them coming and got to his feet, leading everyone in a joyful, if slightly tuneless, rendition of 'Happy Birthday'.

Perched precariously on Scarlet's knee, Emilia bounced up and down in excitement, ecstatic at being the centre of attention. Imperiously ignoring the singing, she held up her arms squealing, 'Dada!' as her sloe-dark gaze fixed adoringly on Tristan.

He handed the open bottle to Nico, putting the other one down on the table so he could scoop his daughter up into his arms where she crowed in delight and pointed at the cake. Across the table Andrei fastened huge, worried eyes on the candle and for a moment it looked as if he might cry. But then Tristan picked him up in his other arm, kissing his dark silky head and murmuring reassurance, and the little face relaxed into a cautious smile.

Scarlet got to her feet with difficulty and came round to stand beside Lily as the singing reached its enthusiastic climax. Nico was circulating with the champagne, pausing beside Dimitri and squeezing his arm as he filled his glass. Holding the two babies in his arms, Tristan knelt down so they were at eye level with the cake. The candles cast a halo of soft golden light on their three faces, making stars dance in their eyes.

Closing her eyes in comical bliss, Emilia pursed her plump rosebud mouth and blew extravagantly. Scarlet clapped her hands with delight, blinking back tears. 'Don't forget to make a wish!' she cried.

Across the table Tristan looked up, and his gaze met Lily's. The candles guttered and died, but his eyes still shone with love.

'I don't need to,' he said with quiet, ironic emphasis. 'It's already come true.'

HARLEQUIN *Presents*

Coming Next Month

from **Harlequin Presents**® EXTRA. Available January 11, 2011.

#133 THE MAN BEHIND THE MASK
Maggie Cox
From Rags to Riches

#134 MASTER OF BELLA TERRA
Christina Hollis
From Rags to Riches

#135 CHAMPAGNE WITH A CELEBRITY
Kate Hardy
One Night at a Wedding

#136 FRONT PAGE AFFAIR
Mira Lyn Kelly
One Night at a Wedding

Coming Next Month

from **Harlequin Presents**®. Available January 25, 2011.

#2969 GISELLE'S CHOICE
Penny Jordan
The Parenti Dynasty

#2970 BELLA AND THE MERCILESS SHEIKH
Sarah Morgan
The Balfour Brides

#2971 HIS FORBIDDEN PASSION
Anne Mather

#2972 HIS MAJESTY'S CHILD
Sharon Kendrick

#2973 GRAY QUINN'S BABY
Susan Stephens
Men Without Mercy

#2974 HIRED BY HER HUSBAND
Anne McAllister

REQUEST YOUR FREE BOOKS!

HARLEQUIN *Presents*®

2 FREE NOVELS PLUS
2 FREE GIFTS!

PASSION GUARANTEED SEDUCTION

*Harlequin Romance author Donna Alward is loved
for her gorgeous rancher heroes.*

*Meet Wyatt as he's confronted by both a precious
little pink bundle left on his doorstep and his neighbor Elli
who's going to show him the ropes....*

Introducing
PROUD RANCHER, PRECIOUS BUNDLE

THE SQUAWKING QUIETED as Elli picked the baby up, and Wyatt turned around, trying hard to ignore the feelings of inadequacy as Darcy immediately stopped fussing.

"Maybe she's uncomfortable. What do you think, sweetheart?" Elli turned her conversation to the baby.

"What do you think is wrong?" Wyatt asked, putting the coffee pot back on the burner.

A strange look passed over Elli's face, one that looked like guilt and panic. But it was gone quickly. "I couldn't say," she replied.

"But you were so good with her this afternoon." Wyatt put his hands on his hips.

"Lucky, that's all. I just...remembered a few things." The same strange look flitted over her features once more.

Wyatt took the coffee to the table. "You fooled me. You looked like you knew exactly what you were doing." So much so that Wyatt had felt completely inept. A feeling he despised. He was used to being the one in control.

Elli and Darcy walked the length of the kitchen and back. After a few moments, she admitted, "I haven't really cared for a baby before. The things I thought of were simply things I'd heard about. Not from experience, Mr. Black."

Her chin jutted up, closing the subject but making him

want to ask the questions now pulsing through his mind. But then he remembered the old saying—*Don't look a gift horse in the mouth*. He'd benefit from whatever insight she had and be glad of it.

"I don't really know what babies need," he said. "I fed her, patted her back like you did, walked her to sleep, but every time I put her down…"

Wyatt almost groaned. Of course. He'd forgotten one important thing. He'd been so focused on getting the formula the right temperature that he'd forgotten to check her diaper. Not that he had any clue what to do there either.

Pulling calves and shoveling out stalls was far less intimidating than one tiny newborn.

"She's probably due for a diaper change, isn't she." He tried to sound nonchalant. This was a perfect opportunity. Elli must know how to change a diaper. He could simply watch her so he'd know better for the next time.

Instead, Elli came around the corner of the counter and placed Darcy back in his arms. "Here you go, Uncle Wyatt," she said lightly. "You get diaper duty. I'll fix the coffee. Cream and sugar?"

Oh boy, Wyatt thought, looking down into Darcy's pursed face, his smug plan blown to smithereens. He was in for it now.

Will sparks fly between Elli and Wyatt?

Find out in
PROUD RANCHER, PRECIOUS BUNDLE

Available February 2011 from Harlequin Romance

Try these Healthy and Delicious Spring Rolls!

INGREDIENTS	DIRECTIONS
2 packages rice-paper spring roll wrappers (20 wrappers)	1. Soak one rice-paper wrapper in a large bowl of hot water until softened.
1 cup grated carrot	2. Place a pinch each of carrots, sprouts, cucumber, bell pepper and green onion on the wrapper toward the bottom third of the rice paper.
¼ cup bean sprouts	
1 cucumber, julienned	
1 red bell pepper, without stem and seeds, julienned	3. Fold ends in and roll tightly to enclose filling.
4 green onions finely chopped— use only the green part	4. Repeat with remaining wrappers. Chill before serving.

Find this and many more delectable recipes including the perfect dipping sauce in

YOUR BEST BODY NOW
by
TOSCA RENO
WITH STACY BAKER
Bestselling Author of
THE EAT-CLEAN DIET®

Available wherever books are sold!